LOVE'S ABIDING JOY

LOVE'S ABIDING JOY

JANETTE OKE

Pickering Paperbacks

Copyright © 1983 by Janette Oke

First published in the USA by Bethany House Publishers,
Minneapolis, USA
First UK edition published in 1985
by Pickering & Inglis Ltd,
3 Beggarwood Lane,
Basingstoke, Hants RG23 7LP,
United Kingdom

British Library Cataloguing in Publication Data
Oke, Janette
  Love's abiding joy.
  I. Title
  813'.54 (F)   PS3565.K35

ISBN 0 7208 0666 6

Printed and bound in Great Britain by
Anchor Brendon Ltd, Tiptree, Essex

Dedicated with love
to my second sister, Jean Catherine Budd,
with thanks for the many times she
has been my extra pair of hands
and for her open heart and open home
that always make me welcome;
and to Orville, the special guy
she brought home
to the family.

Prairie Romances by Janette Oke

Love Comes Softly
Love's Enduring Promise
Love's Long Journey
Love's Abiding Joy

Once Upon a Summer
When Calls the Heart

JANETTE OKE was born in Champion, Alberta, during the depression years, to a Canadian prairie farmer and his wife. She is a graduate of Mountain View Bible College in Didsbury, Alberta, where she met her husband, Edward. They were married in May of 1957, and went on to pastor churches in Indiana as well as Calgary and Edmonton, Canada.

Janette's husband is professor at Bethel College, Mishawaka, Indiana. As well as maintaining the family home for their four children, three boys and one girl, she is active in the Women's Missionary Society. She also serves as a Sunday school teacher in her local church. This is Janette's ninth book.

Contents

Chapter One

Family

"Good mornin'."

The words came softly to Marty; she opened her sleep-heavy eyes to identify the source. Clark was bending over her, smiling, she noticed. Clark did not normally awaken her before he left for the barn; and Marty stirred, fighting sleep in an effort to understand why he was doing so now.

"Happy birthday."

Oh, yes, today was her birthday, and Clark always wanted to be the first one to greet her on her special day. Marty pulled the covers back up to her chin, planning to close her eyes again, but she couldn't resist answering his smile.

"An' you woke me jest to remind me thet I'm another year older?"

"Now, what's bein' wrong with gettin' older? Seems to me it's jest fine—considerin' the alternative," Clark teased.

Marty smiled again. She was fully awake now. No use trying to get back to sleep again.

"Fact is," she said, reaching up and running her hand

through Clark's graying hair, "I don't think thet I'm mindin' this birthday one little bit. I don't feel one speck more'n a day older than I did yesterday. A little short on sleep maybe," she added mischievously,"—but not so much older."

Clark laughed. "I've heard tell of people gettin' crotchety and fussy as they age . . ." He left the sentence hanging; then he leaned over and took any sting from the words with a kiss on Marty's nose. "Well, I'd best get me to the chorin'. Go ahead, catch yerself a little more shut-eye, iffen ya want to. I'll even git yer breakfast—jest this once."

"Not on yer life," interjected Marty hurriedly. "I'd hafta clean up yer mess in the kitchen."

Clark left, chuckling to himself, and Marty stretched to her full length beneath the warmth of her handmade quilt. She wouldn't hurry to get up, but Clark's breakfast would be waiting when he returned from the barn.

Today is my birthday, Marty's thoughts began. Though she wasn't *feeling* older, it seemed, suddenly, that there had been many birthdays. Forty-two, in fact. *Forty-two*. She repeated the number mentally in an attempt to get the feel of it. *Funny, it really doesn't bother me a bit*. No, there was nothing traumatic about this birthday—not like thirty had been, or forty. My, how she had hated turning forty! It seemed that a body must be near worn out by the time one reached forty. Yet here she was, forty-two, and in all honesty she felt no older than she did when she had reached those other two such monumental milestones.

Forty-two, she mused again but did not dwell on the number for long. Instead she thought ahead to the planned events of the day. Birthdays meant family. Oh, how she loved to have her family gathered about her! When the children had been little, she herself had been the "maker-of-birthdays." Now they were grown up and old enough that it was her turn to have a special day. Nandry had served the birthday dinner last year, Clae had reminded them. Marty couldn't really remember. The years had a tendency to blur in together, but, yes, she was sure that Clae was right.

Today being a Saturday, the dinner would be held at the

noon hour instead of in the evening. Marty liked it better that way. They had so much more time with one another instead of trying to crowd in the celebration between the return of the school children and the milking of the cows and other farm chores. Today they had the whole afternoon ahead of them for visiting and playing with the grandchildren.

Just thinking about the promises of the day filled Marty with excitement. Gone all thought of sleep, she threw back the covers, stretched on the edge of the bed, and moved to the window. She looked out upon a beautiful June morning. The world was clean and fresh from last night's rain shower. What a beautiful time of year! There was still that lingering feeling of spring in the air even though many plants had grown enough already to make one know that summer was really taking over. She loved June. Again she felt a thankfulness to her mother for having her in this delightful month.

Marty's thoughts returned to her own children. Nandry . . . Nandry and her little family. Nandry had four children now, and what a perfect young mother she made. Her Josh teased about their "baker's dozen," and Nandry did not even argue against his laughing remarks. Yes, Nandry, their adopted Nandry, would have made her natural mama proud. And then there was Nandry's sister Clae, their second adopted daughter—Clae and her parson husband Joe. Clae too loved children, but Marty felt—though Clae had not said so—that she secretly hoped the size of their family would not grow too quickly. Parson Joe still dreamed about and planned toward getting more seminary training. Marty and Clark added little amounts to the set-aside canning jar which was gradually accumulating funds to help pay for the much-wanted schooling. Marty hoped that they would soon be able to go. Joe and Clae had one little girl, Esther Sue.

Marty's smile left her face and her eyes misted as she thought of their next daughter, Missie. Oh, how she missed Missie! She had thought it was gradually supposed to get easier over the years of separation from loved ones, but it had not been so. With every part of her being Marty ached for Missie. *If only . . . if only*, she caught herself thinking again; *if only I*

could have one chat—if only I could see her again—if only I
could hold her children in my arms—if only I could be sure
that she is all right, is happy. But the "if-onlys" only torment-
ed her soul. Marty was here. Missie was many, many days'
journey to the west. Yet how she longed for her Missie. Though
Missie was not bone of her bone nor flesh of her flesh—Missie
being Clark and Ellen's daughter—Marty felt that Missie was
hers in every sense of the word. The tiny baby girl with the
pixie face who had stolen her heart and given life special
meaning so many years ago was indeed *her* Missie. *Oh, how I*
miss you, little girl, Marty whispered against the pane as a
tear loosed itself and splashed down on the window sill. *If*
only—but Marty stopped herself.

Across the yard moved Clare and Arnie. They were men
now, and yet in spite of the years, there was still much of the
little boy in each of them. Many folks—those not aware of the
death of Marty's first husband—were surprised by the difference in their appearances. Clare looked and acted more and
more like his father Clem—big, muscular, teasing, boyish.
Arnie was taller, darker, with a sensitive nature and finer features like Clark. By turn they loved one another, teased one
another, fought with one another, couldn't live without one
another. Laughing now as they came in for the milk pails,
Clare, who usually did most of the talking, was telling Arnie of
some incident at last night's social event. Arnie didn't care
much for neighborhood socials, but Clare never missed one.
Arnie joined in with his laughter at Clare's description of the
mishap, but Marty heard him exclaim over and over, "Poor ol'
Lou! Poor ol' Lou. I woulda' nigh died had it been me." Clare
didn't seem to feel any sympathy for "poor ol' Lou." He was
wholeheartedly enjoying the telling of the story. As the boys
neared the door, Marty turned away from the window and
dressed slowly. There was still lots of time to get the breakfast
on. They were just now going to milk.

Marty combed her long hair back and lifted the softness of
it. It was still heavy and full. She had sometimes noted the
thinness of the hair on many older women and secretly pitied
them. Well, she didn't have any need to worry on that score

yet. In fact, her hair had really not shown much gray either. Not like Clark. His hair was quite gray at the temples and was even generously sprinkled with gray throughout. *On him it looks good—rather distinguished and manly*, she thought.

Marty dawdled as she pinned up her hair, still examining her thoughts carefully one by one. A birthday was a good time to do some reminiscing. At length, her hair in place, she made up the bed and tidied the room.

As she left her bedroom, the smell of morning coffee wafted up the stairs to her. *Surely Clark didn't carry out his teasing*, was her first thought. No, she had just seen Clark down by the far granary. Marty sniffed again. Definitely it was coffee, and fresh-perked too.

Her curiosity now fully aroused, Marty picked up the fragrance of frying bacon and breakfast muffins. She hurried into the kitchen, her nose fairly twitching.

"Aw, Ma. It was s'posed to be a surprise!"

It was Ellie.

"My land, girl," said Marty, "it shore enough was a surprise all right! I couldn't figure me out who in the world would be a stirrin' 'bout my kitchen this early in the mornin'."

Ellie smiled. "Luke wanted ya to have it in bed. I knew thet we'd never git thet far without ya knowin', but I thought thet maybe I could have it ready by the time ya came down."

Marty looked at the table. It was covered with a fresh linen cloth and set with the company dishes. A small bowl of wild roses was placed in the center, and each plate and piece of cutlery had been carefully assigned to its place.

"It looks to me like ya are 'bout ready. An' it does look so pretty, dear. Those there roses look so good thet I think I could jest sit an' feast my eyes 'stead of my stomach an' not be mindin' it one little bit."

Ellie flushed with pleasure. "Luke found 'em way over at the other side of the pasture."

Marty buried her nose in the nearest rose, smelling deeply of its fragrance and loving it in a special way because it was given to her in love by a caring family.

"Where is Luke?" she asked when she straightened up.

"Don't think thet I'm to be tellin' thet," answered Ellie, "but he's not far away an' will be back in plenty of time fer breakfast. Ya like a cup of coffee while we're waitin' fer the rest to git here?"

"Thet'd be nice." Marty smiled. Instead of merely a birthday girl, she was beginning to feel like a queen.

Ellie brought Marty's coffee and then returned to the stove to keep her eye on her cooking. Marty sipped slowly, watching her younger daughter over the rim of the cup. Had she realized before just how grown up Ellie was? Why, she was most a woman! Any day now she might be taking a notion to cook at her own stove. The thought troubled Marty some. Could she stand to lose another of her girls? the last one? *How lonely it will be to be the only woman in my kitchen!* Ellie had kept life sane and interesting in the years since Missie had left. What would Marty do when Ellie, too, was gone? Why, just the other day, Ma Graham had remarked about what an attractive young woman Ellie had become. Marty, too, had noticed it, but secretly she had been hoping that no one else would— not for a while yet. Once people began to notice and to whisper, there would be no turning back the clock. Soon their parlor would be buzzing with young gentleman callers, and one of them would be sure to win Ellie's heart. Marty was about to allow some tears to spill over when the men came in from the barn. Clare was first. "Hey, Ma, you don't look so bad, considerin'—" he teased, then laughed at his own absurd joke as though it were something really funny.

Arnie looked embarrassed. "Aw, Clare, nothin' funny 'bout yer dumb—"

But Clare slapped him noisily on the back and declared good-humoredly, "Ma, ya forgot to have 'em give this kid of yers a funny bone when they made him up. Don't know how to laugh, this kid."

Clare's teasing then turned to his sister. "Hey, it still smells all right. Haven't ya got to the burnin' stage yet?"

Ellie laughed. She was used to Clare's teasing. Besides, she doted on her oldest brother and he would have done anything in the world for her. Clare roughed her hair and went to wash for breakfast. Ellie tried to pat her hair back in its proper place and then dished up the scrambled eggs. Arnie, content to wait his turn at the washbasin, finally crossed to Marty. "Happy birthday, Ma," he said, laying his hand on her shoulder.

"Thank ya, son. It sure has had it a promisin' start."

"An' soon we'll all be headin' for Clae's. Boy, those kids of Nandry's git noisier ever'time thet we see 'em. 'Uncle Arnie, give me a ride.' 'Uncle Arnie, lift me up.' 'Uncle Arnie, help me.' 'Uncle Arnie—' "

"An' you love every minute of it," cut in Ellie.

Arnie did not argue, only grinned. Marty agreed with Ellie: Arnie did love the kids.

Clark came in then, drying his hands on a towel, and glanced around the kitchen.

"Well, it 'pears thet my family has 'bout gathered in. Everyone waitin' on me?"

"Yeah, thought you'd never git here, Pa," said Clare, taking the rough farm towel and winding it up to snap at Arnie.

"The boys jest now came in," Ellie informed her pa, "so I guess you haven't kept anyone waitin' any."

The men, finished with their washing and fooling around, took their places at the table. Marty moved her chair into position and Ellie brought the platter of hot bacon from the stove. Marty looked at the empty place. "Luke," she said. "Luke isn't here yet."

"Still sleepin'?" asked Clare, knowing that Luke did enjoy a good sleep-in on occasion.

"He'll be here in a minute," said Ellie. "I think thet he'd like fer us to jest go ahead."

"But—" Marty protested, and just then the screen door banged and in came Luke, his hair disheveled by the wind and his face flushed from hurrying. Marty's heart gave a skip at the sight of her "baby." Luke was her gentle one, her peacemaker and dream-builder. Luke, fifteen, was smaller than the other boys and had serious and caring soft brown eyes. Marty felt that she had never seen another person whose eyes looked as warm and compassionate as her little Luke's.

"Sorry," he said under his breath and slid into his place at the table.

Clark just nodded, but his love for his boy showed in his simple nod. "Would you like to wash?"

"I can wait until we pray; then the food won't be gittin' cold."

"Reckon the food will wait well enough. Go ahead."

Luke hurried from the table, inspecting his hands as he went. They were covered with red stains. He was soon back, and the family sat quietly as Clark read the morning scripture portion and then led in prayer.

His prayer of the morning included a special thanks for the mother of the home and his helpmate over the years. Clark reminded the Lord that Marty was truly worthy of His special blessing. Marty remembered an earlier prayer, so long ago when she was a hurting, bewildered and reluctant bride. Clark had asked the Father to bless her then too. God had. She had felt Him with her through the years, and these dear children about her table were evidence of His blessing.

After the prayer ended and the food was passed, Clare looked up at Luke between bites of bacon and eggs. "So, little brother. What ya been up to so early in the mornin'?"

Luke squirmed a bit. "Well, I jest wanted ma to have some strawberries fer her birthday breakfast, but boy—were they little and hard to find this year! Guess it ain't been warm enough yet." He held out a small cup of tiny strawberries.

Marty's throat constricted and her eyes filled again with tears. Her sleepyhead had crawled out early to get her some birthday strawberries. She remembered back to when Missie had first started the tradition of "strawberries for Ma's birthday breakfast." After Missie had left, the children had pooled their efforts for a few years; and then, with the breaking of the pastureland that had housed the best strawberry patch, the tradition had drifted away. And now little Luke had tried valiantly to revive it again.

Clare reached over and roughed his younger brother's hair. His eyes said, "You're all right, ya know that, kid," but his mouth was too busy with Ellie's breakfast muffins.

"Ya should have told me," Arnie whispered. "I'd a helped ya."

Marty looked around the kitchen at the four children still sharing their table, and her heart filled with joy and overflowed with love reflected in the glisten of tears in her eyes.

Chapter Two

Birthday Dinner

"Thet was a lovely dinner, Clae," Marty remarked, delicately catching the last traces of birthday cake crumbs from her lips with the tip of her tongue. Clare's groan as he held his full stomach was eloquent. Josh laughed.

As the plates were pushed back and second cups of coffee were poured, the pleasant clamor of visiting began. It seemed that everyone had something to say all at once, including the children. Clark held up his hands for silence and finally drew the attention of the group.

"Hold it," he chuckled, "ain't nobody gonna hear nobody in all this racket. How 'bout a little organization here?"

Nandry's oldest, Tina, giggled. "Oh, Grandpa, how can one org'nize chatter?"

"Can I go now? Can I go play with Uncle Arnie?" Andrew interrupted, the only boy in the family of Nandry and Josh.

"Just before we all leave the table and scatter who-knows-where, how about if we let Grandma open up her birthday gifts?" asked Clae.

"Oh, yes! Let's. Let's!" shouted the children, clapping their hands. Presents were always fun, even if they were for someone else.

Grandma Marty was given a chair of honor and the gifts began to arrive, carried in and presented by various hands. The children shared scraps of art work and pictures. Tina had even hemmed, by hand stitch, a new handkerchief. Nandry and Clae, presenting gifts from their families, laughed when they realized that they had both sewn Marty new aprons. Clare and Arnie had gone together and purchased a new teapot, declaring that now she could "git rid of thet ol' one with the broken spout." Ellie's gift to her mother was a delicate cameo brooch, and Marty suspected that Clark had contributed largely to its purchase. Luke was last. His eyes showed both eagerness and embarrassment as he came slowly forward. It was clear that he was just a bit uncertain as to how the others would view his gift.

"It didn't cost nothin'," he murmured.

"Thet isn't what gives a gift its value," Marty replied, both curious and concerned.

"I know thet you always said thet, but some folk—well— they think thet ya shouldn't give what cost ya nothin'."

"Ah," said Clark, seeming to realize what was bothering the boy, "but the cost is not always figured in dollars and cents. To give of yerself sometimes be far more costly than reachin' into one's pocket fer cash."

Luke smiled and seemed to feel more at ease as he pushed his clumsy package toward Marty.

"Ya said thet ya liked 'em, so—"

He shrugged and backed away so that his mother could open her gift.

Heavy and bulky, it was wrapped in brown paper and tied at the top with store twine. Marty could not imagine what kind of a gift could come in such a package. She untied the twine with trembling fingers and let the brown paper fall stiffly to the floor. Before her eyes were two small shrubs, complete with roots and part of the countryside in which they had grown. Marty recognized them at once as small bushes from

the hill country. She had exclaimed over them when she had
seen them in full bloom one summer when she and Clark had
taken the youngsters into the hills for a family outing. How
beautiful they had looked in their dress of scarlet blossoms.
She caught her breath in a little gasp as she visualized the
beautiful shrubs blooming in her own garden.

"Do you think thet they'll grow okay, Pa?" Luke's anxiety
showed in his voice. "I tried to be as careful as I could in diggin' 'em up. Tried to be sure to keep from hurtin' the roots
an'—"

"We'll give 'em the best possible care an' try to match their
home growin' conditions as much as possible," Clark assured
Luke; then he continued almost under his breath, "—iffen I
have to haul their native soil from them hills by the wagon-
load."

Marty couldn't stop the tears this time. It was so much like
Luke. He had traveled many miles and had gone to a great
deal of work and care in order to present to her the shrubs that
he knew she loved. And yet he had stood in embarrassment before his family, his eyes begging them to please try to understand his gift and the reason for his giving it. She pulled him
gently to her and hugged him close. Luke wasn't too fond of
motherly kisses in public places, so Marty refrained from em-
barrassing him further.

"Thank you, son. I can hardly wait fer them to bloom."

Luke grinned and moved back into the family circle.

All eyes then turned to Clark. It had become traditional
that the final gift to be given at family gatherings was always
from the head of the home. Clark cleared his throat now and
stood to his feet.

"Well, my gift ain't as pretty as some thet sit here. It'll
never bloom in years to come either. But it does come with
love, an' I hope it be somethin' thet truly gives ya pleasure. No
fancy package—jest this here little envelope."

He handed the plain brown envelope to Marty. Marty
turned it over in her hand, looking for some writing that would
indicate what she was holding. There was nothing.

"Open it, Gran'ma," came a small voice, echoed by many
others.

Marty carefully tore off one corner, slit the envelope open, and let the contents fall into her lap—two pieces of paper and on them words in Clark's handwriting. Marty picked up the first. Aloud she read the message, "This is for the new things that you be needing. Just let me know when and where you want to do the shopping."

"Ya should have read the other one first," interjected Clark.

Marty picked up the second slip of paper. It read, "Arrangements have been made for tickets on the train to Missie. We leave—"

Tickets to go to Missie! All of Marty's thoughts and longings centered on their daughter so many miles away. The recent "if onlys" crowded in around her. She was going to see Missie again. "Oh, Clark!" was all she could manage, and then she was in his arms sobbing for the wonder of it—the pure joy of the promise the tickets held.

When she finally could control herself, she stepped back from Clark's embrace. With a happy smile but trembling lips, Marty said apologetically to her family, "I think thet I need me a little walkin' time, an' then we're gonna sit us down an' talk all 'bout this—" She did well to get that far without more tears, and she left the cozy kitchen filled with the family she loved and walked out into the June sunshine.

Here at Clae's there was no place in particular to go, so she wandered aimlessly. She found herself yearning for the familiar trees and little spring behind her own house. She had gone there so many times over the years when she had some thinking to do. Well, Clae's trees would suffice. Marty certainly did have some thinking to do. She tried to collect her scattered, excited thoughts. She was going to Missie! She and Clark would travel those many miles on the train. No wagons—no slow days of wind and rain. Only padded seats and chugging engines eating up the distance between her little girl and herself. Oh, she could hardly wait! She held up the note that she still held in her hand and read it again. "Arrangements have been made for tickets on the train to Missie. We leave as soon as you can be ready to go. Love, Clark."

As soon as you can be ready to go. Oh, my. There was so

much to be done. So many things to prepare and take with them. There was her wardrobe. She would need new things for traveling. Why, her blue hat would never do to wear out among stylish people, and her best dress had a small snag near the hem that still showed even though she had mended it carefully. *Oh, my.* How would she ever—? And then Marty remembered the second note. "This is for the new things that you be needing. Just let me know when and where you want to do the shopping." "Oh, my," Marty said aloud. Clark had thought of everything, it appeared. "Oh, my," she repeated and quickly changed directions back to Clae's kitchen. She must talk to the girls. They were far more aware of the present fashion trends, and they knew what stores carried the needed articles, and they knew where she would need to go to do her shopping and when the stages ran between the towns. "Oh, my," she said again in a flurry, "I do have me so much to do. Oh, my."

Chapter Three

Planning

The days that followed were busy ones for Marty. Nandry and Clae went shopping with her for yard goods in their small town and then pored over design sketches that Clae made in an effort to achieve fashionable gowns. It was finally concluded that a trip to a larger center would be necessary if Marty were to be presentable to the outside world on a cross-country train trip. But when could she work that into this busy time? Though her wardrobe consumed much of Marty's time and attention, there were other matters that weighed heavily on her mind as well. One of them was the fact that Clare had wedding plans. As yet, the definite date for the marriage had not been set, but how could they go way off west not knowing? Marty held her tongue, but she did try to "plant the seed" in Clare's thinking that it would be most helpful if his young lady could finalize a date. Clare understood the subtle suggestion and told Marty he would see what he could do.

Marty was also anxious about her packing. Every day she thought of something new that surely Missie and Willie and their young family might need. How much dare she accumulate before the train company—or Clark—would declare that she had far too much baggage? She sighed as she tried to select the most important items.

Clark occasionally tried to draw from Marty an estimated day for departure. She knew that a decision must be made. Clark had many responsibilities of his own that needed to be assigned to others. He couldn't properly sort them out until Marty had given him some kind of idea as to when she would be ready to go. She didn't know whether to hope that Clare would set the wedding date for immediately or postpone it until they were sure to be back.

Then, of course, there were the other children. True, Ellie was capable of caring for the household, but it seemed like a big job to put on such slender shoulders. Marty conveniently forgot that at Ellie's age she had already been a married woman.

Yet Marty's heart was most concerned for Luke, her gentle youngest. How she wished that she could take him with her. At the same time, she was afraid to suggest it, even to Clark. What if Luke did go, and what if he decided that he liked Missie's West, and what if he decided not to come back when Clark and Marty returned home? No, she'd best leave Luke safely where he was. She had no desire to have another child so far away from home.

So Marty spent her days musing and fretting. She tried not to let it show, but it did. Each of the family noticed it and finally decided that something needed to be done or Marty would wear herself out. Nandry and Clae made arrangements for the care of their children and planned a trip to the city by local stagecoach for shopping. Ellie was invited to go along. The necessary items were purchased and prepared for travel. Marty was afraid she was spending an inappropriate amount of Clark's money, but she did rather enjoy this unusual extravagance. She purchased a few pretty things to take to Missie as well. Who knew whether Missie had had opportunity to shop at all since leaving her home?

Clare discussed his marriage plans with his sweet Kate and, with the help of her mother, they were able to arrive at a suitable date. They wisely agreed that a hurried wedding would not be a good start for their marriage, so August 27 was chosen. Clark and Marty would have no problem being home by then. Clare and Kate planned to live in Clark's first little log home, so Clare would spend the intervening time preparing the place for occupancy, and Kate would spend her time on new curtains and floor rugs.

Ellie asked many questions and advice on the running of the home and the tending of the garden—questions to which she already knew the answers, but she knew that it would help her mother depart with greater peace of mind if she explained it all again. Ellie assured Marty that she was looking forward to the experience, and Marty felt that it might truly be an adventure for the girl. Nandry and Clae promised to lend a hand if ever she needed assistance.

Luke took to making subtle comments on the coming separation. He suggested that it would be good for all of them to spend some time on their own and learn some independence. He pointed out to Marty that he would be spending most evenings studying for the entrance exams for college the coming fall and he would have very little time for socializing even with family members; the additional quiet of the house during their absence would be very helpful in giving him extra study time. Marty sensed that he was trying to put her mind at ease about going off and leaving him, and she appreciated his concern.

Many times a day Marty went through the mental sorting of what she wished to take. She eyed her garden, her canned goods, her sewing materials, her chicken coop—she even eyed the milk cows. She shook her head. How in the world would she ever decide? At length, she knew that she could never be sensible, so she asked for help from her family in the final decision. Eventually it was narrowed down to a list over which Clark did not mournfully shake his head.

At length Clark was given the go-ahead. He could set a date for departure. It seemed that within a few more days, Marty could be ready to go.

"When are ya leavin'?" asked Ma Graham when they had a minute together after the church service.

Marty was relieved that she actually had a date.

"Well, we take the stage out from town on Wednesday, and go on over to catch the train out of the city the next mornin'," she replied.

"Ain't ya excited?" Ma asked, but didn't need nor wait for an answer. "My, I miss thet girl of yourn so much myself thet I can jest imagine how yer feelin'. Give Missie a big kiss an' hug fer me. I have a little somethin' here thet I want ya to take on out to her. I didn't dare send nothin' big—ya havin' so much of yer own stuff to tend to, so I jest made her a little lace doilie fer her table."

Marty hugged Ma warmly, the tears shining in her eyes.

"Missie will 'preciate it so much," she said.

And so the packing of the crates, cases, and trunk was done; the clothes for travel carefully laid out; and the scattered items and thoughts collected. Many last-minute instructions, some necessary and some only for Marty's sake, were given to the three boys and Ellie. There was some measure of assurance in just reviewing them over and over.

Clare and Arnie had been farming right along with Clark for a number of years, so Clark had no doubts about their ability to care for things. They each had a piece of their own land to farm now, too, but they could handle it all in Clark's absence. They had been instructed to get help if ever they needed it, and Luke was anxious to be all the help that his studying time would allow.

It was understood without actually being discussed that Luke probably would never be a farmer. He had a very keen mind and a sensitive spirit and was presently leaning toward the idea of being a medical doctor. Clark and Marty felt he would be a great honor to them as a doctor, but Luke was not pushed for a commitment on his future.

And so the farming was left to the boys and the kitchen to Ellie. Marty knew that she was quite able to care for the needs of the brothers; still Marty fretted some as she thought of all the work ahead for the young girl.

The day of their departure dawned clear and bright. The warm sunshine spilled down upon the waking world. Marty was up even before Clark and, in her excitement, flitted about caring for last-minute things that really needed no attention. Her efforts were not totally without value, for it did give her something to do until it was time for them to load into the spring-seated wagon and head for town.

Their four children from home accompanied them, and when they arrived—too early—at the stagecoach offices, Nandry and Josh and their family, and Clae and Joe and Esther Sue were already there.

The excitement was felt by everyone and resulted in too many talking at once, too much nervous activity, and too many near-wild children. Clark grinned at the whole tension-filled bunch of them and called a halt to the bustle of activity and noisy chatter.

"Whoa," he called, lifting up his hand, his signal for quiet. "How 'bout we see iffen we can git a little order out of this confusion?" Everyone stopped mid-sentence and mid-step and then began to laugh.

"I suggest," went on Clark, "thet we go on over to the hotel an' have us a cup of coffee an' a sandwich. Be a heap quieter, an' we still have lots of time to kill before this here stage is gonna be leavin'." Eventually they all fell into line and headed for the hotel and the promised coffee. Josh broke line, whispered to Nandry and then fished in his pocket.

"Tina, yer ma says it be okay fer ya to take those here little ones over to the General Store fer a candy treat. It being a special day, how 'bout ya all git *two* pieces of yer favorite kind."

Shouts of approval answered him, and he passed Tina the coins. She took Mary and Esther Sue by the hands and headed for the promised treat. Andrew disdained holding hands and marched off on his own. Baby Jane was content to be held in her mother's arms and to put up with the grown-ups while they visited over coffee cups.

When they finally were seated and had placed their orders, the talking did become a bit more orderly. They even waited for one another to finish their sentences before breaking in. Marty knew that her churning stomach had no interest in a sandwich. She ordered a cup of tea and sipped at it now and

then between her involvement in the talk and laughter. The
men ordered sandwiches and even pieces of pie to go with
them. Marty wondered fleetingly how they ever managed it,
only a few hours since they had downed a big breakfast.

Departure time seemed to be in no hurry to come. The food
had been eaten; the cups drained, replenished, and drained
again; the same admonitions given and repeated; and the
same assurances spoken over and over. Marty fidgeted in her
seat. Clark at last said that he supposed they could go on out
and check on the progress of the stagecoach.

As they stood chatting before the stagecoach office, Zeke
LaHaye, Willie's pa, joined them. He greeted them all with
one nod and sweep of his hat, then reached to shake Clark's
hand.

"Guess I needn't tell ya how I be a-envyin' ya. Sure would
love to head on out with ya. Always had me a-hankerin' to see
the west country, an' with my boy out there it sure does git
awfully hard to jest hold myself here at home sometimes."

"Well, now," said Clark, "ya jest ought to throw in yer
bedroll an' come along."

Zeke answered with a smile. "Sure do be temptin'. Did
bring this here little parcel iffen ya be thinkin' thet ya can find
a little room fer it someplace. Hate to be a-botherin' ya like,
but it jest ain't possible to let ya go without sendin' somethin'
along fer my family."

"No trouble. No trouble a'tall," assured Clark and placed
the parcel with the growing stack of their belongings.

Marty looked at the big pile of "things" going west. There
were all of their own daily necessities, the many things they
had packed to take to Willie and Missie, the added articles
from Clae and Nandry, the gifts from Ma Graham, Wanda
Marshall, Sally Anne, and some from Missie's students during
her teaching days. Yes, the pile had grown and grown and, indeed, each additional item meant "more trouble," but she
would have no more denied Zeke LaHaye the pleasure of sending something to his family than she would have denied herself. She'd discard her hatbox if necessary in order to make
room.

The stage finally appeared, two minutes early, and all of the baggage and crates were loaded. Zeke's package fit in too, and Marty was able to take even the hatbox.

Over and over the words, "Ya tell Willie . . ." or "Give Missie . . ." or "Kiss them for me" were echoed from their loving family members. Marty turned to each one with tears in her eyes and pounding heart. It was so exciting to finally be on their way; if only "good-byes" didn't need to come before one had the pleasure of "hellos." She kissed Luke one last time, gave Ellie one more hug, threw kisses to the many-times-kissed grandchildren, and hurried forward lest the stage pull away without her.

The good-bye shouts followed them on down the road. Marty leaned from the window for one last wave before the coach turned the corner, and then she settled back against the already warm seat.

"I do declare," she remarked seriously to Clark, "I do believe thet travelin' be awful hard work. I feel all worn out like."

"We've barely started travelin', Marty," Clark laughed softly. "It's not the travelin' thet has ya all tuckered. It's the gettin' ready and the excitement. From now on, ya have nothin' to do but jest rest."

Marty smiled at Clark's calm assessment but looked rather doubtful. How could she ever rest when her whole body vibrated with excited energy? Well, she'd try. She'd try.

Chapter Four

The City

It seemed to be an awfully long, dusty, warm stagecoach trip to the big city where they would catch the train. At least in their own farm wagon, they could catch the breezes and stop to stretch their legs. The morning sun moved up high in the sky and beat down unmercifully. The open windows helped a little. The other three passengers were men. Clark talked to them some, but Marty had little interest in the conversation. Besides, her mind was on many other things. In spite of the warmth in the stagecoach, Marty knew that a stylish traveling lady did not remove her hat, even in the heat of the day; but how she longed to slip hers from her warm head and let it lay in her lap.

They stopped to change horses and to allow the passengers a few moments to walk around a bit. Marty was glad for the relief. Then on they went again, bumping over the rough tracks of the road. Marty had assumed from looking that the road was rather smooth and rutless; but the stage wheels seemed to find bumps enough.

At noon hour another rest stop was taken, and Marty crawled stiffly down with Clark's assistance and sought out the shade of some nearby trees. The men scattered in various directions to walk, sit, or stretch out on the cool grass.

Marty took her little lunch bag with her and spread out a noonday meal of sandwiches and cool drink with tarts and cookies for dessert. Marty herself wasn't much interested, but Clark was. It appeared that the traveling was not adversely affecting his appetite.

All too soon the stage was ready to move on again. They left the coolness of the trees and took their places on the hot, dusty leather seats. The minutes of the afternoon were ticked off by the grinding and bumping of the wheels and the steady rhythm of the horses' hooves. Occasionally, a hoot or shout from the driver would call some new order to the teams.

In spite of herself, Marty found her head nodding. The heat, the inactivity, and the fact that she had been missing some of her sleep all helped to make her drowsy. But it was hard to sleep comfortably in the jostling wagon; as soon as she would begin to slip into relaxing slumber, another bump or shake would snap her awake. It was worse than no sleep at all. She shifted her position and fought to remain awake.

A change of teams at another stagecoach station broke up the monotony of the afternoon. Marty's back and legs ached, and she was thankful for the stretch. She thought of Missie's long journey west by wagon train and more fully appreciated their courage through the discomfort of it all.

It was almost suppertime when the stagecoach pulled into the city station. Marty leaned forward to eagerly see all that she could as they traveled the busy, crowded streets, then checked herself. She was *not* acting like a lady, and she settled back against the seat and allowed only her eyes to peer out of the shallow window.

After alighting, Marty walked around, flexing her muscles and observing all of the strange sights and sounds, as Clark collected their belongings and made the proper arrangements for everything to be on the morning's train west. All they took with them now were two cases and Marty's hatbox. Marty felt a bit panicky as she watched all of their luggage being carted away. Was the man truly dependable? Would he be *sure* to put them on the right train? Would everything arrive safely? Was it all properly labeled? What would they ever do if it did not make it?

But Clark seemed to have no such fears. Seemingly relieved and confident that he had all things cared for, he took her arm.

"Well, Mrs. Davis," he teased, "here we are in the big city. What shall we be doin' with it?"

"Doin'?" asked Marty blankly.

"Well, they say thet a big city is full of all manner of excitin' an' forbidden things. Ya be wishin' to go lookin' fer some of 'em?"

Marty looked shocked.

"Me?"

Clark laughed at her literal interpretation. "No, not you. An' not me either. I'm jest funnin' ya. I have heard thet they have some very good eatin' places, though. I could sure use me some good food. Somethin' about sandwiches thet don't stay with a man fer long. Ya interested?"

"I reckon," replied Marty, though in secret she found herself far more interested in what the people would be wearing than in what they ate.

"Well, let's jest find us a hotel room to git settled an' leave our belongin's, an' then we'll see what we be a-findin'."

They found a hotel quickly enough. It was the biggest one Marty had ever seen. She looked around her at the high, ornate ceiling, the glistening hanging lights, and the elaborately paneled doors. *This must cost nigh on to a fortune*, she thought, but she did not voice her opinion to Clark.

Clark was handed a key to a room and given a few instructions, and then he took Marty's arm and they began to climb the stairs—many of them. Marty did not count them as she climbed. She was much too busy studying the attractive paper on the walls and the colorful carpeting beneath their feet. At length, Clark stopped before a door and used the key. He pushed the door open and then stood to the side to allow

Marty to enter. The room before them was the most elegant
Marty had ever seen. She looked about her, studying carefully
every detail. She wanted to be able to describe everything in
the room to her daughters.

The wallpaper was a richly patterned blue and the draperies were deep blue velvet with thick fringes. The bedspread,
heavy and brocaded, had a cream background with some blue
threads interwoven. The ornate chest appeared to have been
hand-carved, and there was a special stool or small table on
which one rested his cases. The imported carpet was a riot of
rich purples, crimsons, blues, and golds, all blended together
in an attractive overall pattern. Marty took it all in and then
turned to Clark.

"My," she said, then again, "My, I never be a-knowin' thet
all of this grandness be possible."

"I jest hope thet this 'grandness' has a comfortable bed,"
he responded, crossing over to the bed and testing it for softness. "I'm a-thinkin' thet before mornin' I'll likely be pinin'
fer the 'grandness' of my own four-poster."

Marty, too, felt the bed. "Feels fine to me," she stated,
"though I'm admittin' to feelin' so tired thet a plank floor
might even be welcome."

Clark laughed. "Before ya settle fer thet plank floor, let's
go see what this here town has to offer an empty stomach."
And, so saying, he attempted to lead her from the room.

"Whoa now," argued Marty. "Iffen I'm gonna dine out like
a fine lady, I'm gonna need to freshen up first. Goodness
sakes, the stage was so hot an' dusty one feels in fair need of a
bath an' hairwash."

It took Marty longer to prepare for going out than it did
Clark. He waited patiently while she primped and fussed and
finally felt confident enough to venture forth. They descended
the stairs slowly, and Clark made inquiry as to the location of
a nice dining room. Assured that the one in the hotel was one
of the finest the city had to offer, they proceeded into an im-
mense room with elaborate columns and deep wine-colored
draperies. Marty had never dined in such splendor. She could
scarcely take her eyes from the room and its occupants long

enough to properly select from the menu. Everything on the stiff card before her looked too fussy, too much, and too expensive. It was hard for her to make up her mind. She wished that she could find something simple like fried chicken or roast beef. Clark asked for the house specialty and, without checking to see what it was, Marty echoed his order.

She tried not to stare, but the people moving about the room and sitting at the white-covered tables seemed to be from another world. She had to take herself consciously in hand and insist that she remember her manners. Still, she was relieved and pleased to notice that she did not stand out in the crowd as "backwoods" or "frumpish." Her daughters had chosen her clothes well. How thankful she was for their knowledge and encouragements.

The meal was delicious, though there was far too big a portion served; Marty, who was not used to wasting anything, had a difficult time leaving the food on her plate and sending it back to the kitchen. She was concerned, too, that the cook might take offense and feel that the food had not pleased her. After she had eaten all she could and pushed back her plate, she still was not sure exactly what she had eaten. It had been very tasty—but not identifiable like her homecooked farm suppers of roast beef, potatoes and gravy. Everything about the city was different.

They ordered French pastries to go with their coffee and lingered over them, enjoying the taste, the atmosphere, and the pleasurable luxury of sitting with no responsibility to hasten them away from the table.

When they felt that it would be impolite to remain any longer, they rose from the table and returned to the lobby. Clark purchased a local paper and tucked it under his arm as they again made their way up the stairs to their room. Marty held her skirt carefully as she climbed; it would never do to step clumsily on her skirt and damage such an expensive hemline.

"So how do you plan on spendin' this lazy evenin', with no mendin' or sewin' in yer hands?" Clark asked, as he opened the door to their room.

"Isn't botherin' me none," responded Marty. "As tired as I be feelin', I expect thet sleep sounds 'bout as good to me as anythin' thet I could be doin'."

Clark smiled. "Go on. Tuck yerself in then. Me, I'm jest gonna check the paper an' see what's goin' on in the world."

Marty prepared for bed and crawled between the cool, smooth sheets with a contented sigh. Oh, how tired she was! She longed for a good long sleep. She would be off before you could say—. But she wasn't. Try as she might to relax in the big, soft bed, her mind still kept whirling. She thought of Missie and the family that she was going to see; she thought of Ellie, Luke, Arnie, and Clare back home. Was there anything that she had forgotten to tell them, any reminders that she hadn't given, any instructions that she had missed? Would the baggage really make it on the train? What would it be like sharing the close proximity of a train car with strangers for days on end as they traveled? Marty's mind buzzed busily with questions.

Clark finished reading his paper, prepared for retiring, and slipped in beside her. Soon Marty heard his soft breathing and knew that he slept in spite of the hotel bed. Still sleep eluded her. She stirred restlessly and wished for morning. Once they were actually on that train and headed for Missie's, she was sure that *then* she could relax.

Chapter Five

Alarm

In spite of a restless night, Marty roused early the next morning. Anticipation took charge of her once again, driving her from the bed. Clark stirred as Marty threw back the blankets.

"Rooster crow already?" he teased, then shut his eyes again and turned over.

Marty didn't let his joshing bother her but went about her morning preparations. She had already decided on the dress and hat she would wear for their first train ride and carefully worked out the wrinkles with the palms of her hands. She shook out the hat, fluffing up the feather, and stepped back to admire the plume. *My, this is some hat,* she thought. She felt a mite self-conscious about wearing it but then assured herself that all of the fashionable ladies wore them.

Marty dressed carefully and then began packing her nightclothes and her gown of yesterday in her case. The gown smelled dusty and looked bedraggled from the stagecoach ride. *What a shame to pack it away in such a mess!* she fretted. She wished there were some way to freshen it first. She selected a few pages from Clark's newspaper and carefully wrapped the dress in it. Clark seemed not the least disturbed by the crackling newspaper.

Marty finished all there was to do, and Clark still hadn't stirred. She wasn't sure what she should do. She hated to waken him, but what if they were late and missed their train? She had no idea of the time. She crossed to where Clark's vest hung on the back of a chair and fumbled in his breast pocket for his pocket watch. *It isn't there!* Marty's mind flashed to each of the terrible stories she had ever heard about the big city. They were true! Someone must have come into their room in the dead of night and stolen Clark's watch. If his watch was gone, what else had they taken? Marty hurried to her case. Was her cameo from Ellie still there? And what about the gold brooch that Clark had given her two Christmases ago?

Marty had packed them on the very bottom of the suitcase. Carefully now she lifted each item from the case, going down on her knees on the floor to lay things out all around her. When she remembered the hours she had spent carefully packing each item of her clothing, she could have cried. Would she ever get them so neatly arranged again? Many of the gowns she had folded in thin tissue wrap supplied by the dress shops in which she had made her purchases. And now, as she lifted them out, no matter how hard she tried to be careful, she disturbed the garments and wrinkled the tissue. Yet she *had* to know—she had to know if her few items of precious jewelry had been stolen along with Clark's watch. Clark would be so disappointed! His three sons had gone together to purchase the gift for his last birthday, and he had proudly worn the watch chain across his chest.

Marty stopped suddenly in the middle of her search. Perhaps she shouldn't be wasting precious time now. Perhaps she should run down to the front desk and report the loss. Maybe there was a chance to still catch the thief. No, first she must know how many missing things to report. So Marty continued unpacking her case, item by item, laying each one around her in one of the neat piles on the deep blues, golds, wines and scarlets of the carpeted floor.

Marty was almost to the last item when Clark roused from sleep, stirred himself and lifted his head. At first he thought that he must be seeing things. He had seen Marty carefully pack her suitcase in just such a manner only a few short days ago. Was she really packing *again*? Clark shook his head to clear it of the cobwebs of the night. Marty remained as before, lifting each item—and she was taking them *out* of the case!

"Ya repackin'?" Clark asked mildly, and Marty jumped at the sound of his voice.

"Oh, Clark!" she cried. "I'm so glad thet yer finally awake. We've had us thieves in the night." Marty's hands hurried on, emptying the last few items from her case.

"Thieves?"

"Thieves!"

"What ya meanin', *thieves*?"

But Marty interrupted him with a glad cry. "Oh, they're still here! Oh, I'm so glad, so glad."

Clark was out of bed by then, looking down on his wife who clasped her precious jewelry to her bosom.

"Look!" she cried. "They didn't find 'em."

"Who find what? I'm not a-followin'—"

"The thieves—the thieves who stole yer watch. Oh, Clark, I'm so sorry. I know how much ya loved thet watch an'—"

"Ya meanin' this watch?" Clark asked, lifting it from the small table by the bed.

Marty gasped.

"Ya found it."

"Found it? I never lost it. I put it there by my bed so's I could check the time in the mornin'."

"Oh, Clark. I checked in yer pockets fer it, an' when I couldn't find it I thought thet someone had—"

But Clark had started to laugh. He pointed at Marty and at the empty case and the heaped-up clothing and held his sides as he laughed uproariously.

At first his outburst miffed Marty, not as yet over her concern and fear during the trying ordeal of the last several minutes. Then she looked about her at the mess that she had created and the watch held dangling from its chain in Clark's hand, and the humor of the situation struck her also; she buried her face in her hands and laughed with Clark.

When she finally had control of herself again, she gasped out, "Well, if this isn't 'bout the dumbest thing thet I've ever done. Jest look at me! I think thet my sleepless nights have really numbed my brain. Oh, Clark, jest look at the mess thet I got here!"

Then a new thought struck her. The repacking of the case was going to take some time if she were going to do it carefully. Perhaps she would need to stuff things into the case and run to catch the train. Nervously, she looked up, her hands quickly returning things to their proper places.

"How much time we got 'fore—"

Clark, understanding the worry in her eyes, assured her that they had far more time than she would ever need for the repacking, even though she was particular and fussy as Aunt Gertie. Marty had never learned any more about Aunt Gertie, but when Clark wanted to make a point of someone's fussiness, he always brought up Aunt Gertie. The boys had taken up the phrase too, though Marty knew for sure that they knew nothing of the mysterious Aunt Gertie.

Marty, relieved that there was plenty of time, carefully set out to put everything back in its proper place while Clark shaved and dressed.

She was still laboring over the open case when Clark stood, hat in hand, all ready to go.

"Be it time?" Marty inquired.

"Take yer time—we still got lots of it. Soon as yer ready we'll go on down an' find us some breakfast. A man can't travel on an empty stomach. Then we'll come back on up an' pick up our things." Clark tipped up Marty's chin and looked into her face with a smile. "Guess we might as well do the rest of our waitin' at the train station. I have me a-feelin' thet yer not gonna rest easy until yer sure thet yer gonna be on thet there train," he added.

Marty packed in the last few items and closed the case.

She stood to her feet and nodded her head. There was no use denying what Clark had just said. He knew her far too well.

"I'm ready now," she said. "An', yes, I could be usin' some breakfast."

Clark offered his arm, checked his safe-in-hand watch, and chuckled again.

Chapter Six

The Journey Begins

At the train station, Marty was sure she had never seen so many people all in one place. Her eyes and ears were busy picking up the new sights and sounds all around her. Clark found a bench on which she could wait and went to make final arrangements for their journey. Marty was content to sit and watch. She had never seen such an array of strange and colorful dress. Why, even the menfolk looked like they belonged on the pages of some storybook!

Even though they still had lots of time before the train was due to leave the station, Clark had been right: Marty would not really rest easy until she was actually seated on the train and assured that its engine was pulling them westward. So, in spite of her interest in the crowd, she fidgeted and was glad when she saw Clark moving back across the room.

A rather bold-looking woman with bright copper hair and a broad-brimmed, scarlet-plumed hat sat across from Marty. To Marty's surprise, the red-haired woman also noticed Clark. The woman peeked out at his approach from under long, kohl-darkened lashes and watched Clark approach. Then Marty saw the woman slyly and deliberately drop a glove at her own feet and pretend to again busy herself with the book that she held before her face. As Clark reached the "lost" glove, he bent, gentleman-like, recovered it, and then glanced around to see who its owner might be. Marty saw the redhead steal a very small peek, and then her eyelashes began to flutter; Marty knew that she was about to make her presence known to Clark in some cute little speech.

Marty stood up quickly and spoke before the lady in the hat had time to open her mouth. "Everythin' set, Clark? Oh, a glove. Perhaps it belongs to you, ma'am." Marty turned to the redhead with a very sweet and winning smile. "It matches your hat perfectly."

The lady accepted her glove without comment. Marty moved away, taking Clark's arm and steering him to a seat nearer the exit door. *I can't imagine the brazenness of these city women,* she was declaring inwardly. *They'd steal a woman's husband right out from under her very nose. Why, thet's even worse than takin' a watch!* Clark remained unaware of the small commotion.

Someone finally called, "All aboard for points west," and Marty quickly stood and shook the wrinkles from her skirt and straightened her hat. Clark gave her arm a reassuring squeeze and they moved with the crowd toward the waiting train.

Marty, having never been on a train before, was both excited and apprehensive. She found the high steps awkward to maneuver with her long skirts and was glad for Clark's helping hand as she climbed up.

Inside the train car, the rows and rows of seats were not as elegant as Marty had imagined they would be. The plush fabric was faded and even a little frayed in spots. Marty assumed that the fancier trains would run between the large eastern cities.

They were jostled a bit as they sought for a seat. Everyone seemed to be in a hurry to find a place, as though they were afraid the train might leave without them. Clark and Marty found a seat quickly enough. They settled themselves and tucked their carry-along luggage under the seat. Marty sighed deeply. They had made it. Now if only she could get a glimpse of the sun to make sure that this train was pointed in the right direction.

Gradually the commotion around them began to subside as other passengers selected seats as well. Marty noticed that they were in very mixed company, though not too many women had boarded the train. The men appeared to be of every type and class—from businessmen to cattlemen, from miners to farmers like themselves, drifters and youngsters running away from home.

Marty shuddered inwardly as the scarlet plumes moved down the aisle and the red-headed woman, with skirts hoisted and eyelashes fluttering, took a seat. She had selected a spot far from the other womenfolk in the car, among the men who had already pulled out a deck of cards and made themselves a makeshift table. Great drifts of cigar and cigarette smoke already blurred the air around them. Marty hoped there would be no smokers in her area, but it was a vain hope. Not being used to smoke at all, Marty found it particularly trying. Were they to endure this all the way to Missie's? Already she felt about ready to choke, and they hadn't even left the station yet.

The train gave a long, low sound like an anguished groan, and the squeaking wheels began to revolve slowly. They were on the way at last. To Marty's chagrin, she still couldn't tell if they were headed in the right direction.

Gradually the train began to pick up momentum. The rough-looking buildings on the back streets of the town moved past them hurriedly now. Marty watched carriages and horsemen pulled up on side streets waiting for the train to pass by. Some of the horses stomped and reared, not liking one bit the angry-sounding, smoke-blowing engine. Children called and waved, and dogs barked; but the train moved on, unresponsive to it all.

They left the town behind and moved out into the open countryside. Marty could not draw her gaze away from the window. Trees swished by them; cattle lifted tails and ran off

46

bawling; horses snorted and swung away, blowing angrily, tails and manes flying. Still the train pounded on, wheels clickity-clacking and smokestack spewing forth great billows.

It's a wonder, thet's what it is, thought Marty. *Why, I bet we're goin' 'bout as fast as a horse can gallop, an' nobody needs to lift a finger fer the doin' of it.*

The crewman stoking the firebox was, fortunately, unaware of Marty's thoughts. Had he known of them, he would have been glad for an opportunity to show her whose muscle and hard work made possible the forward speed of the train.

Marty finally took her eyes from the passing countryside long enough to look at Clark. She was interested in his reaction to this new experience. To her amazement, she found that Clark had settled himself comfortably and, with head leaning back against the makeshift package of their lunch bundle, he slept soundly as though sleep was the full purpose of a train ride.

"Well, I never," mumbled Marty under her breath and then smiled. She should be sleeping, too. The past few days had been most trying, and the sleep that she had gotten in the last few nights was limited indeed. Clark was wise. He too was tired. He needed the rest. She'd try as well. But, in spite of her resolve, she could not as yet get her body to relax. She'd just watch the scenery for a while. Maybe she could sleep later.

Marty must have slept, for she aroused at the sound of a crying baby. It took her a few moments to get her bearings, and then excitement again filled her as she recalled that they were on the way to Missie.

The baby continued to cry. Marty opened her eyes and turned toward Clark, when she remembered that he had been sleeping, too. She didn't want to disturb him if he hadn't wakened yet. But when she looked, he was not there. For a moment, she was unnerved. Where could one disappear to on a moving train? Remembering the "lost-watch" scare of the morning, she told herself that Clark would not be far away and not to get in a dither.

The coach was even more blue with smoke than it had been when she had dropped off to sleep. It was hot and stuffy, too, and Marty longed for some fresh, pure air. She gazed about her at the crowded coach. The poker game was still going on at the far end of the car. The redhead had removed her brilliant hat, and she no longer sat alone. A distinguished gentleman in a fancy suit and frilly shirt was sitting with her. They laughed a lot as they talked.

The crying baby was in the seat across the aisle. The poor mother already looked tired out. She had two other little ones as well. The man who accompanied her growled to her to "hush the kid 'fore we git throwed off the train," and the woman tried even harder. The baby was not to be placated. The man got up and, muttering to himself, left angrily. This started another one of the children crying, and the young mother really had her hands full. Marty moved to leave her seat and go to the woman's aid, but a matronly looking woman arrived first.

"Can I help you some?" she asked, and, without waiting for a reply, she took the crying baby. "You care for your son, and I'll try to get the baby to sleep."

Marty's heart went out to the young mother, and she said a quick prayer of thanks for the kind, motherly soul who was helping.

The baby soon was sleeping. Marty wondered if perhaps the young mother had bundled her too tightly and the poor little infant was nearly smothering in the discomfort of the sun-heated coach.

Marty laid aside her own hat and tried to fan her flushed face. *What I wouldn't give to be able to go fer a walk*, she thought. *Sure would feel good to have a little wind on one's face.*

Clark returned. Marty's relief showed in her eyes.

"Feelin' a little better?" Clark asked.

"I did sleep some, an' it sure didn't do me no harm. Would be nice to cool off a mite. This here coach is so stuffy an' so filled with cigar smoke, I feel like I was a-travelin' in a saloon 'stead of a—"

"Now what you be knowin' 'bout a saloon?"

"I don't, it's jest—" But Clark was laughing at her.

"Where ya been?" asked Marty to change the conversation.

"Jest stretchin' my legs some. Ain't much of a place to walk, thet's fer sure. Jest back an' forth, back an' forth. S'pose it helped a little."

"What I wouldn't give fer a walk 'bout now," said Marty.

"Ya want fer me to ask 'em to stop the train an' let ya off fer a spell?"

"Clark . . ."

Clark stopped his teasing.

"What time is it, anyway?" asked Marty.

Clark pulled out his pocket watch.

"Well, it's almost noon. Quarter of twelve, in fact."

Marty sighed heavily. "Thought thet it would be at least late afternoon," she said. "Seems like we been travelin' fer half of forever already."

Clark smiled.

"How many days did ya say we'd be on the train?"

"Reckon they didn't say fer sure. They was rather offhand about arrivin' time. Said thet the trip usually took 'bout a week—dependin' on the weather, the track, an' such."

"A week! I'm a-thinkin' thet we'll have us enough of this train by the time thet week is over."

"Well, now, I didn't say *this* train, exactly. This train we leave in three days' time. We transfer to another one. This one is usually on time to where it's a-goin'. It's the one further on thet's some changeable."

"I didn't know thet we would be usin' another train. What'll it be like?"

"I'm not rightly sure. Only thing I know, it seems a bit unpredictable. But it won't be so bad. By the time we board her, we'll already be in the West an' almost there."

Marty suddenly felt hungry. "Anythin' still fittin' to eat in thet there pillow of yourn?"

Clark passed her the lunch. It hadn't suffered much. Ellie had packed it well.

Marty lifted out a box that held sandwiches. "Sure would be glad fer a nice hot cup of tea or coffee," she commented.

"I think thet I might be able to find some," and Clark left his seat, walked down the aisle and out the swinging door. He was soon back with two steaming mugs of hot coffee. It was too strong for Marty's liking, but it was coffee and it did wash the smoke taste from her throat.

They finished their lunch with a couple of tarts, and Marty carefully repacked the lunch sack.

"Ya know, ya could stretch yer legs a bit iffen ya like to. Seed other women movin' 'bout some. Little room down thet way."

Marty smiled her thanks and stood up. She couldn't believe how wrinkled her dress looked in just one morning. She tried to smooth the wrinkles out but they stubbornly remained, so she shrugged her shoulders in resignation and moved out into the aisle.

Marty had been vaguely aware of the rock and sway of the train as she sat in her seat, but she had had no idea how decided it was until she took a step forward; the train suddenly seemed to lurch, throwing her off balance. She quickly put out a foot to re-balance herself when the train rolled the other way, leaving her startlingly off-balance again. Each place she went to put her foot was either too high or too low. She felt like a drunken sailor as she wobbled her way down the aisle. At last she gave up trying to make it on her own and firmly grasped the seats as she moved forward. It seemed to be a long walk to the "little room," and by the time Marty had made it back to Clark, she had had enough of train-aisle walking for the time.

The train hooted and chugged, whined and rocked its way westward. Marty viewed more than one sunrise and sunset and was happily content that the train was truly headed in the right direction.

They stopped at small towns to let off or take on passengers. Sometimes the train seemed to sit for a ridiculously long time while train cars were shuffled and shouting men hauled off or on some sort of cargo. At these times Clark and Marty would leave the train and walk, strolling around just to get the kinks out of their muscles. On occasion they visited a store to restock their own little food supply. Often it was no cooler out on the station platform than it had been in the stuffy coach, but at least it was a bit of relief from the cramped position. Marty began to wonder if it really would have been much more difficult to cover the miles in a jolting covered wagon.

The landscape around them changed with each passing day. Trees were fewer in number, often forlornly clumped together by a meandering stream. The towns, sometimes no more than a few scattered houses, were now even farther apart than before. On the third day, they rolled into a town that Clark announced was the place where they would transfer to the other train. Marty was not reluctant to make the change. She had no ties to this present train or its passengers. She had found very little in common with their fellow travelers. Those few whom she had become acquainted with had all seemed to get off at earlier stops except for one middle-aged lady in a dove-gray gown and hat. Mrs. Swanson was heading west to live with her son, her husband having died recently. Marty thought that it was spunky of the little woman to make such a life-changing move all alone.

Clark had visited with several of the men on the train, attempting to learn all that he could about the West before arriving at his son-in-law's ranch. He did not wish to appear to the ranch hands as another "ignorant fella from the East."

When they arrived at their point of transfer and the train dismissed its passengers, Clark and Marty made their way across the rough platform. People milled about and called to one another, but as there would be no one in this town that they knew, they kept their attention on the task of finding their way from the station to a suitable lodging.

Informed that a hotel was just down the street within easy walking distance, they set out. When Clark requested a room from the man at the reception desk, he was told that a room was available; but Marty was shocked when she heard him name the price. Clark did not argue with him but counted out the bills from the small roll he carried in his pocket.

They climbed the worn, carpeted stairs and found their

room number on a door. Marty looked about her, her eyes widening at the sight that confronted them on opening the door. The room was almost bare, except for a good measure of dirt and dust, and the bed looked as though the sheets and pillows had been used by at least one other occupant—maybe more. Marty had little objection to sparse furnishings, but filth was another matter.

Clark noticed the sad state of the room, too. Marty could see him eying the muddy boot prints on the floor and the soiled pillows strewn on the bed. But he made no remark.

"I think thet I'll take a little walk an' sorta check out the town. Ya wantin' to come along, or do you wanna jest rest a bit?" asked Clark.

A walk did sound appealing, yet from what Marty had so far seen of the town, she was not so sure she wanted to walk in it.

"I think thet I'll jest rest me here fer a bit. I'll see the town when we go out to git our supper," she answered.

Clark took his hat and left.

Marty didn't know what to do with herself after Clark had gone. She wished for a pail of hot, soapy water and a good scrub brush. The place looked like it could do with a good washing.

She crossed to the bed with the thought of lying down for a rest, looked at the dirty linen and changed her mind. She walked to the window, intending to pass some time by watching the action down on the street. The window looked out on nothing but the prairie and wind-swept countryside. She lifted her case from the only chair in the room and tried to settle herself in it. It had a broken spring that made it impossible to sit comfortably. Marty decided that her only choice was to pace the floor. Well, she could certainly do with the exercise after being invisibly chained to the swaying train seat for three days. She walked. Round and round she walked, wishing that she had gone with Clark.

About the time she thought she would surely go crazy, Clark returned. Over his arm he carried clean bed linen.

"The maid has arrived," he joshed.

"Where'd ya git thet?" Marty asked admiringly. "Ya been foragin' through hotel closets?" she teased.

"Not exactly. Actually, it wasn't all thet easy to come by. I went on out fer a walk like I said. There be only one other hotel, of a sort, in this here town. It boasted 'bout bein' 'full up.' Couldn't find a decent roomin' house anywhere. So, when I got back here, I jest asked the fella at the desk for some clean linens. I said thet it 'peared like the maid had somehow missed our room when she was a-makin' up. He weren't too happy to 'commodate me, but I jest stood right there, smilin' at 'im an' waitin'. He finally found me some."

Marty was happy to strip the bed and put on the clean sheets and cases.

"Not too much fer eatin' places either," Clark continued as she worked. "Did see a small place down the street. Looks a little more like a saloon than a cafe, but it mightn't be too bad iffen we git there early an' leave as soon as we're done."

"We can go most anytime. I'll jest fix my hair some an' grab me a hat."

They left the hotel and walked out into the brisk wind. Marty held her hat with one hand and her skirt with the other.

"Fella I met says thet the wind blows like this most of the time here," remarked Clark as they leaned into the wind. Marty wondered what in the world the ladies did if they ever needed one of their hands free to carry something.

When they reached the unpretentious building where they were to get their evening meal, Clark held the door against the wind. They seated themselves at a small table, and Clark nodded for the waiter. They soon learned that the "house speciality" was stew and biscuits; or roast beef, gravy, and biscuits; or beans, bacon, and biscuits. They ordered the roast beef and settled down to wait for their meal.

Marty glanced around the room. The lighting, a lone, flickering lamp on each table, was dim. The few windows seemed to be covered with some kind of dark paint. A blue haze from the smoking of the occupants further hindered visibility. Most of those who lounged around were not eating but drinking. Marty did spot three men in the far corner who were having a meal. The others just seemed to be talking or playing cards. Occasionally a loud laugh would break the otherwise comparative silence in the place. At least for now, Marty was the only woman in the place.

Marty hoped that their order would come quickly so they might leave soon. If this was Missie's West, Marty wasn't sure she would be at home in it. She felt uneasy in her present surroundings. Having never traveled beyond her own small community since leaving her girlhood home, Marty was unfamiliar with her present environment. She had seen and heard things on this trip that were entirely new to her. She didn't think she was in favor of a lot of what she saw—the brashness, the intemperate drinking, the gambling, 'the casual attitude toward life and morality.

Their meal arrived. The waiter asked gruffly, "Watcha drinkin'?" as he set the plates down, frowning when Marty asked for tea. She hastily changed her order to coffee before he had time to respond. He didn't fuss about the coffee, but when he set it before her it was so strong she wasn't sure if she'd be able to drink it.

The meat was a little tough and the gravy was greasy and lumpy, but Marty sopped her biscuits in it and ate like the men in the corner. She was unable to finish it all and was relieved when she felt she had eaten enough that she could push back her plate and leave the rest. Clark had a second cup of coffee, and then they were free to go.

Marty was unprepared for the bright sunshine when they stepped out the door. She had forgotten that it was still daylight. She took advantage of the fact to study the buildings of the town and look in the store windows. The items on display did not really seem all that different from what Mr. Emory carried at the General Store back home. The fact both surprised and relieved her. Perhaps Missie was able to shop after all.

It was too early to retire, so Clark suggested a short walk. Marty didn't like the wind but, remembering her confining attempt to walk in the dirty little room, she agreed. They walked on past the remainder of the buildings on the street:

the bank, the sheriff's office, the telegraph office, another store, on past the stagecoach office to the feedstore, the livery and the blacksmith. Clark slowed his steps to better watch the action at the smithy's. Two burly men were shouting and shoving as they prodded a big roan-colored ox into the ox-sling for shoeing. The ox had decided on his own that he didn't need new shoes. Marty heard some words that she didn't think were intended for a lady's ears, so she hastened her steps. Clark lengthened his stride to catch up to her.

Having eventually left the board sidewalks behind, the roadway was dusty and rough, but it felt good to walk full stride. Marty let go of her skirt, allowing the hem to swish the ground as she walked. The wind wasn't as strong now, or maybe she was just getting used to it. She took off her hat, carrying it carefully in her hand, and letting the wind tease at her hair. It felt good, and she wished for a moment that she could reach up and pull the hairpins from it as well and shake it loose to blow free.

They left the street and turned on to a well-worn path. It led them into a grove of small trees; and, after walking for about fifteen minutes, they were surprised to discover a tiny stream that flowed rather sluggishly along. It wasn't like Marty's spring-fed crik back home, but it was water; and its discovery brought rest and joy to Marty's heart. She stooped to pick a few of the small fragrant flowers that grew along its banks.

Clark seemed to enjoy it, too. He stood and breathed deeply. "I wonder jest where it comes from," he murmured, "an' where it goes. This little bit thet we see here before us don't tell us much 'bout it a'tall. It could have started high up in the mountains as a ragin' glacier-fed river and been givin' of itself all across the miles until all thet is left is what we see here. Or it could go 'most from ocean to ocean by joinin' up with cousin waters thet eventually make it a mighty river. Someday it could carry barges or sailin' ships. Rather interestin' to ponder on, ain't it?"

Marty looked at the small stream with a new respect.

They lingered awhile, and then walked much more slowly

back into town. On the way they watched the western sun sink below the far horizon with a gorgeous display of vibrant colors.

"Well," sighed Marty, "I sure do favor me Missie's sunsets."

The hotel room looked just as bleak and bare when they again reached it, but Marty felt much better about having a clean bed. And she was sure enough ready for it now. After two nights on a swaying train, it would be good to have a solid place to lie down. They prepared for bed, prayed together, and crawled between the sheets. Clark put out the light, and before many minutes had passed Marty knew that he was sleeping soundly. She lay for a while thinking of the family at home and feeling just a bit lonely. Then she thought of Missie and her family, and the lonely feeling slipped away. Soon she too drifted off to sleep.

It was sometime during the night when Marty awoke. Something was wrong. Something had wakened her. Was it a noise of some sort? No, she didn't remember hearing anything out of the ordinary. Clark stirred. He seemed restless too. Marty turned over and tried to go back to sleep. It didn't work. She turned again.

"You havin' problems, too?" asked Clark softly.

"Can't sleep," Marty complained. "Don't rightly know why, I jest—"

"Me, too."

They tossed and turned as the minutes ticked slowly by.

"What time is it?" asked Marty. "Anywhere near mornin'? Might as well git up an' be done with it iffen it is."

Clark reached for his watch. He couldn't read the hands in the darkness.

"Mind iffen I light the lamp to git a look?"

"Go ahead. Lamplight ain't gonna make me any wider awake than I am already."

Clark struck a match and lit the lamp. As the soft glow spread over the bed, Marty gasped. Clark, who had moved the pocket watch into the light to get a look at the time, jerked his head up.

"Bedbugs!" exclaimed Marty.

Both of them were instantly on their feet and many small insects darted quickly for cover.

"Bedbugs! No wonder we couldn't sleep! Oh, Clark! We'll be scratchin' our way all across these prairies."

"Funny," said Clark, "I never felt 'em bitin' me."

"Thet's the way with bedbugs. Sometimes ya don't even feel 'em until the bite starts to swell up an' itch. You'll feel 'em fer sure tomorrow, I'm a-thinkin'."

Marty ran to check their cases and thankfully noted that they were tightly closed. Only their bodies and the clothing about the room to worry about.

"Clark, when we leave this here place, we gotta be awful sure thet we don't take none of them with us."

"An' how we gonna do thet?"

"I'm not rightly sure. One thing I do know—thet light stays on fer the rest of the night, an' I'm not crawlin' back into thet bed."

They washed carefully, then inspected each item of their clothing before they put it on. Marty brushed and brushed and brushed her hair in the hopes that if there were any of the little creatures in her hair, she would brush them out. None appeared. She didn't quite know whether that was a good sign or a bad one.

After checking and rechecking, they packed their belongings carefully and closed the cases tightly. Marty put the cases as close to the lamp as she could and stood vigil. It was still only four o'clock . . . hardly the hour of the morning to take to the street.

They managed to wait until the first rays of the dawn were showing on the eastern horizon, and then they left the hotel. The room had been paid for in advance, so Clark just tossed the key on the desk; the sleeping clerk stirred slightly, murmured something inaudible, and settled back to snoring. They walked through the unpainted doors and out into the street.

"Where are we gonna go?" questioned Marty. "Nothin' will be open yet."

"Well, there's a bench over there in front of the sheriff's office. How 'bout sittin' in the sun fer a spell?"

Marty nodded. It was a bit cool in the morning air; she could do with a little sun. She hoped that the warmth of the rays would reach them quickly.

It was a while before others also were stirring about the streets of the town. The livery hand arrived first and went about the duties of feeding the horses and a pair of mules. Roughly dressed men eventually swaggered out of the hotel, a few at a time; then the blacksmith began pounding on some metal in his shop. Shopowners began to open doors and re-arrange window signs. The sheriff checked his office and then headed for the hotel and a cup of morning coffee. There was more movement toward the hotel, and soon Marty and Clark could smell cooking bacon and brewing coffee. Marty had not realized she was hungry until that moment.

Clark turned toward her. "Rather fun to watch a town wake up. I've never done thet before," he commented, and Marty nodded her head in agreement.

"It's not really so different from home as far as looks goes—yet it 'feels' strange," she answered. "Still, I haven't seen anything—" Her words were interrupted.

Four cowboys rode into view, their horses dusty and tired. They led four other horses behind them with some kind of bundles tied on their backs. The horses were spotted and wore no saddles, although two of them had colorful blankets tossed across their backs. The men rode past silently, their leather-encased feet swinging freely and their hair hanging past their shoulders in long, black braids. Upon observing the braids, Marty snatched a second look. Why, those weren't cowboys. They were Indians! Now *that* was different. The riders looked neither to the left nor the right as they rode down the street and pulled their mounts to a stop before the General Store. They swung down from their horses and began to untie the bundles from the backs of the pack animals.

"Looks like they've got 'em a pretty good catch of furs," observed Clark.

"Furs," said Marty. "I never thought of furs. What kind, ya supposin'?"

"I've no idea. Coyotes, badgers, maybe. Not close enough

to the mountains fer bears or wildcats, I'm a-thinkin'. But then I'm not much fer knowin' jest what they do have hereabouts."

Marty turned only after they had all disappeared.

"Well," said Clark, "ya ready fer some breakfast?" He stood up and stretched his tall frame.

Marty stood too and picked up her lunch bundle and hatbox. Without thinking, she reached to scratch an itching spot on her rib cage, then checked herself; a lady did not go about scratching in public. At the same time, she realized that Clark was scratching his neck. Marty looked at the spot. "Oh, my," she whispered.

Clark looked at her.

"Ya sure enough got yer share," stated Marty. "They're beginnin' to show up all along yer collar."

"Bedbugs?"

"Bedbugs. Well, not the bugs exactly—but where they been."

"Guess they liked me better'n they did you, huh?"

" 'Fraid not," said Marty. "I got me four or five places thet I'd jest *love* to be a-scratchin'."

Clark laughed. "Well, maybe a cup of coffee an' a slice of ham will take our mind off 'em." He picked up the cases and motioned Marty toward the hotel's dining room they had passed up the night before in favor of the saloon place.

"Fella told me thet this ain't the fanciest place around; but it's the only one thet's open this time of the day, so I guess we'll give it a try. Surely nobody can make too much of a mess outa just boilin' coffee."

Maybe Marty was just hungry, or maybe the food actually wasn't so bad; at any rate, she ate heartily.

Chapter Seven

Arrival

The next three days on the slow-moving train were even more difficult for Marty. For one thing, she was in a fever to reach Missie, and the many delays and the hesitant forward crawl irritated her. She was also tired from several nights without a good rest, and the train they rode was even less elegant than the first. The worn seats and cramped quarters made it difficult to sit comfortably, and there was no room for stretching or walking.

There were only two other women on the crowded train, and neither seemed inclined to make new friendships. The men, rough and rugged, appeared to be gold-seekers or opportunists. The constant smoking of strong cigars and cigarettes made Marty feel like she was going to choke. The temperature was getting hotter and hotter, and the heat and the stuffiness of the one passenger car almost overcame her; the bedbug bites did not help her frame of mind. Occasionally there was something of interest out of the train window, like the small herd of buffalo that wandered aimlessly along beside the track, but usually there was nothing at all to see but brown hills and wind-swept prairie. Now and then herds of cattle or a squatter's makeshift buildings came into view. Marty counted only three *real* houses, each surrounded by many outbuildings. She guessed each of these places to be someone's profitable ranch.

The small towns along the route, though few and far between, looked very busy. Marty wondered where the people came from. As much as she normally enjoyed watching people, she did not care for that activity now. She just wanted to get to Missie, and each time that the train stopped and frittered away precious time, Marty chafed inside. What could they possibly be doing to take so long in such an insignificant place anyway? Marty fussed, minding the heat, the cramped quarters, the smoke, the delay, and the itching bites.

But all of her fretting did not get them one mile closer to Missie, she gradually came to realize. At length Marty willed herself to take a lesson from Clark and learn some patience. She settled herself in her corner and determined not to stew. She even decided to study the countryside and see what it might have to share with her.

Early on the third morning, Clark returned from chatting with a fellow in a seat farther up the coach and informed Marty with a grin that the man had said Missie's small town was the next stop; and unless something unforeseen happened, they should be in by noon. Marty was wild with joy. Now it was even harder to sit still and not chafe about the sluggish engine that took them forward at such a snail's pace.

The man was right. Just before the noon hour the train began to slow, and they all stirred themselves and started to gather together their belongings.

Marty cast one final look around at her fellow passengers. She noticed a youth hoist up his small bundle and move toward the door. He looked tired and hungry, and there was a bit of fear and loneliness in his eyes, too.

Why, he don't be lookin' any older than my Luke, Marty thought compassionately. *Suppose he's come on out here all by hisself an' don't know where he's goin' or what he'll find when he gits there.*

Marty was about to ask Clark if there wasn't something they could do for the youngster when the train stopped and the boy disappeared in the crowd.

They climbed down the steps from the train, looked around quickly, and moved toward the dusty new sidewalk. The boards had not fully weathered yet, and they were newer than the town. Marty noticed the buildings were recently built, but many of them looked like they had been constructed in a big hurry and with the cheapest material available; little attention was given to fanciness.

Marty's eyes turned to the scores and scores of bawling cattle milling around in the corrals to the right of the tracks, kicking up dust and drowning out all other noises. Yes, this was a cattle town, to be sure.

Marty was not interested in buildings or cattle—only people. She was busy scanning the crowd for a glimpse of Missie.

Dust-covered cowboys—and equally dust-covered horses—moved back and forth on the main street, wide hats almost hiding the features of their faces. A number of ladies walked by, none of them in hats but wearing cheap and practical bonnets or nothing on their heads at all.

Marty was trying to stay close to Clark through the crushing passengers from the incoming train, all the while straining her eyes for the first sight of Missie, when a deep voice drawled beside them, " 'Scuse me, sir, but do you folks be the Davises?"

Marty looked up at the cowboy who stood beside them, hat in hand.

"Shore are," replied Clark.

"Right glad to meet ya, sir—ma'am. I'm Scottie, foreman for the LaHayes, an' I been sent to meet this here train." Marty felt her heart sink with disappointment. Missie was not here.

Clark set down a case so that he could extend a hand. "Glad to meet ya, Mister Scott."

Scottie did not correct him.

"I'd be happy to take ya on over to the hotel, ma'am, and let ya freshen up some. It's gonna be a bit of a ride to the ranch. Then we'll collect yer things an' be off."

"I'd like thet," replied Marty, and they followed Scottie down the street.

"Mrs. LaHaye is most bustin' with eagerness. She could hardly stand it thet she ain't here to meet ya herself. Never know when this here train is finally gonna pull in. This one was scheduled to be in here yesterday. 'Course, one day late ain't so bad. Sometimes it's been as much as five. A little hard fer her to stand around waitin' with two little ones in tow—ya know what I mean?"

Scottie didn't wait for an answer.

"Boss, he came into town to check yesterday—brought the whole family, jest in case the train happened to be on time. Well, she warn't. He sent me on in today. He was gonna give it another try tomarra. Missus will be right glad thet it won't be necessary."

Marty was glad, too. *Mercy me*, she thought, *I'd a-never stood it if we'd been five days late—and neither would Missie!*

They entered the small hotel, and Scottie spoke to the man at the desk. Marty was shown to a room. It was not fancy, but it was clean. Marty was glad for a fresh supply of water for a good wash. The men left again to go pick up the baggage from the train station. Marty prayed that everything had arrived—and safely.

She couldn't help but feel disappointed and empty. She had thought when she arrived in this little town that her long wait to see Missie would be over. But of course Scottie was right. It would have been very foolish for Missie to make the long trip every day, not having any idea when the train might actually arrive.

The room seemed cool in spite of the warm weather, and after Marty's wash she lay down on the bed, promising herself that she'd just rest for a few minutes while she waited for Clark and Mister Scottie to come.

Clark found her sleeping when he returned and was tempted to leave quietly and allow her to get some much-needed rest; but he felt that she would never forgive him if he did, so he roused her gently and said Scottie was ready to take them in for a little to eat before they headed for the ranch.

Marty was hungry, but she did begrudge even the time spent in eating. They hurried with their dinner, because Scottie too was anxious to get back to the ranch.

Marty sat in the wagon on a seat that had been especially fashioned for her by Willie and made as comfortable as possible. Clark sat up with Scottie. Scottie was not a great talker, but he was generous in answering any questions; Marty paid no attention to the conversation. Nor did she particularly watch the passing scenery. Her mind was totally on Missie, wondering how much reserve the passing years might have put between mother and daughter. Would they still be able to share feelings and thoughts, or would the years and the experiences have closed some doors for them? Marty felt a little fear grip at her heart. And what about Missie's children, her grandchildren? Would they see her as only a stranger they did not particularly welcome to their world? The questions and doubts persisted until her mind was seething with anxieties as they rumbled along. Clark turned back to check on her now and then, and she managed to give him a shaky smile. She hoped he didn't notice her edginess.

And then they came over a hill, and Scottie pulled up the team. "There's the boss's spread, right down there," he said, pride coloring his voice. It was evident that he felt a measure of ownership in the ranch, just by his association. Marty's heart skipped. Right down there! Right before her very eyes was their Missie's home. Marty saw a large, sprawling, gray stone home. Soft smoke curled up from the chimney. Off to one side, she could see a garden and a very small stream flowing away from a rocky embankment. She let her eyes seek out the pen with the chickens, the seeming miles of corrals, the bunkhouse and cookshack, and, yes, there on the other side was a straw-colored mound. *That must be Missie's soddy.* Marty's eyes filled with tears, and she had an impulse to jump from the wagon and run down the hill. Remarkably, she held herself in check; Scottie clucked to the team and they moved forward.

Whether it was Scottie's driving, or Marty's wishful thinking, or the eagerness of the team to return to their stalls,

Marty never knew for sure; but the remainder of the trip down the long, winding hill went more quickly.

At the bottom of the hill, Scottie "whoaed" the horses and handed the reins to Clark. "I'll jest be gettin' on back to my duties," he said. "You'll be a-wantin' to make yer greetin's in private," he added as he stepped down from the wagon.

"And many thanks to ya fer yer welcome an' fer drivin' us this long way," Clark said warmly. Scottie tipped his hat to them and moved off toward the barn. Marty climbed up beside Clark for a better view of the house as the horses moved forward. A flash of red calico in a window, and then . . . there was Missie, her arms opened wide and her face streaming with tears, running toward them calling their names. Marty ran to embrace her beloved daughter. They held each other close, crying and laughing and repeating over and over tender, senseless endearments.

At last, at last, sang Marty's heart. *At last I have my "if only."*

Chapter Eight

Introductions

The hours that followed were wild with excited chatter and activity. The two grandsons had immediately captivated their new-found grandparents. Marty was so thankful they moved forward to them without hesitation and even allowed hugging. Nathan beamed his pleasure. He was all ready to "take over" the entertainment of the two special people in his mother's life. "Mama said I could show ya my room," and "Mama said you'd go ridin' with me, Grandpa," and "Mama said you'd like to see my own pony," and "Mama said you'd read to me sometimes." Missie laughed, and Marty realized that she had been carefully preparing her children for the adventure of meeting their grandparents.

Josiah was too young to be as active in the conversation, but he pulled at coattails and jerked at hands and insisted on "Up!" Marty was thrilled with how quickly the two boys felt at ease with their grandparents. When Josiah did manage to steal a scene from Nathan, he was full of chatter of "See this," and "Do you like my . . . ?" and "Lookit, G'amma." For Clark and Marty, their hearts were captured on sight by two small boys.

The whole house was filled with happy sounds as Missie proudly showed them from room to room. Marty exclaimed over the comfort, the coolness, and the attractiveness of the big stone house. They had entered through wide, double doors into a large, cool hall. The floor was of polished stone, and the inside walls were textured white stucco. Missie had used paintings with Spanish-Mexican influence to decorate the walls and had placed an old Spanish bench of white wrought iron against one wall. The bench had cushions of a flower-print material and Missie had picked up the shade of green in them to highlight little finishing touches in the room, a pleasing and cool effect. The living room was large and airy with a mammoth stone fireplace and deep red and gold fabrics on the furnishings. The draperies, of matching material, were tied back with gold cords. It too looked Spanish *and*—thought Marty—*very rich*. The floor was dark-stained wood, and the walls were, like the entry, textured stucco. Scattered across the polished wooden floors were deep-colored rugs—not the homemade variety but storebought. The pictures and lamps were Spanish—and elegant, with blacks, reds, and golds predominant. Marty viewed in awe. Never had she seen such a room.

On they moved to the dining area. "And," said Missie, with a wave of her hand and a laugh, "that's as far as we've been able to go with our grandness. From here on, it's common livin'. But it'll come, little by little, with each cattle shipment."

Missie gestured toward a long, homemade trestle table which easily seated eight. "Willie has promised me some dining room chairs an' a *real* table this fall." Though the chairs were comfortable enough, they were not matched or of good quality. The white-stuccoed walls were quite bare, and inexpensive curtains hung at the windows. A simple cabinet against the far wall held the good dishes that Marty had insisted Missie take west. Somehow the simple, homey room put Marty's heart at ease; the differences now between them might not be so great after all.

"Oh, Missie, I'm so proud of you and so happy for you!" she exclaimed with a quick hug. Clark's approving grin echoed that sentiment.

The bedrooms were all big and roomy, but, again, the furnishings here were simple and the curtains and spreads and the rugs on the floor were all homemade. Marty recognized many things that she had helped to fashion.

Missie led them to the other wing, the kitchen area of the house. Marty was surprised when Missie stopped at the door and gave a brief rap, then walked in. A wiry little Chinese man was busily engaged in preparations for the evening meal. Marty had not known that Missie had a cook.

"Wong," said Missie, "this is my pa, my mama."

The Chinese man favored them with a big grin and bobbed his head up and down as he acknowledged the introductions.

"How'do, how'do," he said over and over. "Wong pleased with pleasure. How'do, how'do."

Clark and Marty both answered with smiles.

"Wong is trying hard to learn our difficult English," Missie explained while Wong beamed at them. "He has done very well in a short time. He does not need to learn how to cook. He knew all about cookin' when he came. Every rancher hereabouts envies us and hopes for an invitation often to eat his delicious food."

Wong bobbed his head again with pleasure and led them around the large kitchen. Marty had never seen so much working room. The stove was big, too, and Wong proudly lifted the covers from several steaming kettles, all sending forth delicious odors.

Missie led her parents down a hall and toward a back door.

"I had me no idea thet ya had a cook. My, my," remarked Marty.

"Wong has not been with us for long," Missie answered. "At first, I thought that Willie was being silly to suggest it, but I wonder now why I even tried to fight it. Wong is so much help. He helps with the laundry, too. It gives me more time for the children, and I still have plenty to keep me busy with this big house. I'm glad that we have him—an' it gives him a job an' a home as well. Nathan and Josiah adore him. But it made

Cookie terribly jealous at first," Missie continued. "He was so afraid that someone else would take his place with our boys. But the two rascals have managed to keep both of the men happy. Actually, the two cooks seem to really enjoy one another now. Most evenings they get together for a cup of coffee and a chat. In fact, Cookie is the one who volunteered to teach Wong English."

Missie's long speech had brought them to the patio at the back of the house. The front, the bedroom wing on the one side, and the kitchen wing on the other, surrounded this lovely area on three sides. The fourth side looked out toward the spring beyond Missie's flower beds. When Marty remarked on their beauty, Missie informed her that they were all flowers she had taken from the neighboring hills, except for the bed of roses. Scottie, a little red-faced, had presented her with them when he had returned from purchasing some choice livestock farther south.

The sheltered veranda between the patio and the house was shaded and cool even in the late-afternoon heat. Marty imagined what a pleasant place this would be to spend an afternoon sewing or reading to the children. She was very impressed with the home that Willie had built for Missie. She was pleased with their good taste, and she admired Missie's choice of color and texture in the rich-looking "new" area of the house. Also, it said to Marty that times were good, that Missie and Willie were making upward strides in their standard of living. The homier, simple furnishings in the remainder of the house also spoke to Marty. These told her that they were willing to wait, to build gradually, to not demand everything at once, showing maturity and good judgment. Marty *was* proud of them—both of them.

After the look through the house, Willie invited Clark out to see the barns and stock, and Missie took Marty to show her the garden, the spring, her chickens and the little soddy.

The boys were now frustrated. Nathan, who clung to Grandma's hand, didn't like to leave her to go with the men, but he was most anxious to show off his pony. Josiah, who had been riding on Grandpa's shoulder, hated to climb down but did not want to get too far away from his mother. Besides, he absolutely adored the chickens! After some complaints from both of the children, the three "men" headed for the barn, and the women and the younger son took the path to the garden.

Marty was pleased at the sight of Missie's garden. True, it wasn't as far along as her own had been on the farm back east, but the plants looked healthy and productive and Marty could see that many good meals would be coming from the little patch.

The water from the spring was not as ambitious as the spring back home, but the effect that it had on the area surrounding it outweighed the difference. All around were brown hills and wind-swept prairies, but here near the spring were green growing things and small, shivering-leafed trees—truly an "oasis."

Missie briskly led the way to the chicken pen. Forty or fifty hens squawked and squabbled in the enclosure. They looked healthy enough, and Missie assured her mother that they were very good egg producers.

Josiah immediately began hollering at the chickens, attempting to throw handfuls of grass and dirt at them through the wire. Since the wind was blowing from the wrong direction, most of it blew right back into Josiah's face, so Missie put a stop to the activity. Josiah was quick to obey, blinking dust from his eyes.

As they moved on toward the unassuming soddy, Marty noticed that Missie referred to it with love and even joy, a fact that Marty found very difficult to understand. Missie pushed open the rough wooden door and they entered the dim little sod shack. When Marty's eyes had adjusted, she could make out the bed in the corner, the black iron stove that still remained right where it had been, the small table and the two stools.

Marty gazed all around her, from the simple furnishings to the sod roof and the packed-dirt floor.

This is the "home" that waited for you after that long, hard trip? An' ya actually lived here, Marty thought incredulously. *Ya actually lived in this little shack—an' with a baby! How could ya ever do it? How could ya stand to live in such a way? My, I . . .*

But Missie was speaking: "Willie wanted to tear it down, to get it out of here, but I wouldn't hear tell. Got a lot of memories, this little place. We've had to re-sod the roof a couple of times. Roofs don't last too long with the winter storms, the wind an' rain; an' once they start to leak, they aren't good for anything."

Marty did not express her feeling about the soddy. Instead she expressed her feeling for her girl. "I'm so proud of you, Missie—so proud. I hoped to bring ya up to be able to make a happy home fer the one thet ya learned to love. An' ya did. Ya looked beyond these here dirt walls into the true heart of the home. Home ain't fancy dishes an' such, Missie. Home is love and carin'. Remember when I insisted on those fancy dishes, Missie? I said thet you'd be so glad fer them someday. So I fussed 'bout ya takin' 'em even though ya really had no room fer 'em an' could have taken somethin' more sensible in the room thet they took in the wagon. Well, I was wrong, Missie." Marty's hand touched her daughter's cheek. "I was wrong, an' you were right. Home ain't dishes, frills, an' such, Missie. Home is love an' carin'. You showed me thet ya could truly make a home an' ya could do it with jest yer own hands an' yer own heart. I'm proud of ya. So very proud."

Missie's answering smile was understanding as Marty wiped the tears from her eyes. She looked around once more before leaving the small sod shack; this time it did not look as bleak, nor the floor as earthy. In those few short minutes, something had happened which changed the appearance of the little room.

Chapter Nine

Catching Up

When the children were finally tucked into bed after insisting on a story from both Grandma and Grandpa, Clark and Willie had gone to his office, a small room off the kitchen, to discuss the business of farming and ranching. Missie and Marty settled comfortably in the living room with coffee cups.

"It was useless to try to 'catch up' before this," said Missie, "but I think that things are quiet enough now for us to talk—really talk. I have so many questions. I just want to know 'bout everyone—everyone. I hardly know where to start, but you might as well start talkin', 'cause I just can't bear to let you go to bed until I find out all 'bout those at home."

Marty drew a deep breath. "I've been jest 'bout dyin' to tell ya all 'bout the family. My, ya'd be surprised, could ya see yer brothers an' sister now!"

"Is Clare still the tease?"

"Worse . . . worse, seems to me. He's always funnin' and I sometimes wonder iffen he'll ever grow up. Yer pa says he will, once he marries an' settles down."

71

"An' what is his Kate like? Clare wrote me. Sounded in the letter as though she was nothin' less than an angel sent from heaven. What's she really like?"

"Kate's a fine girl. We feel thet she's jest what Clare needs. She's quiet and steady, a little overly cautious at times, but they should balance one another real well. She's quite tall, with brown hair, large violet eyes . . . I think thet it was the violet eyes thet caught Clare's 'tention. Though she's not what ya'd call a beauty, she does have very pretty eyes."

"An' you said that they're gonna marry this fall?"

"August 27. Might have been a little sooner, but we wanted to be sure and have lots of time to get home ag'in and git us ready fer the big event."

"Does Arnie have a girl?"

"He's been callin' on a little gal over in Donavan County. You remember Arnie; he's rather shy. He takes things pretty slow-like. Ellie says thet Hester will need to do the proposin' iffen it ever gits done!" Marty chuckled. "I think thet Arnie jest hasn't quite made up his mind yet. Wants to be good an' sure. She's a nice little girl, but her brothers are rather no-goods. Have a bad reputation in the area. Arnie ain't 'bout to let thet influence him, but he feels thet it's important when one marries they accept all of the family members."

"Sometimes that just isn't possible," remarked Missie.

"Well, Arnie feels thet with Hester it has to be. She is very protective of her brothers. Would fight fer 'em if necessary. Arnie admires thet in her. But he wants to see the good in 'em that Hester sees. So far," Marty laughed softly, "I think thet he's been hard put to find some good, even though he's sure been lookin'."

"I hope he doesn't spend too many years *lookin'* and let some girl with no such problems be snatched up by someone else in the meantime."

Marty sighed. "Arnie deserves a good girl. He is so sensitive to the feelin's of others. He's got a lot of his father in him, thet boy."

"What 'bout Ellie? She got a beau?"

"Not really. Not yet. Guess I was sorta hopin' thet ya

wouldn't ask. I keep tryin' to pretend thet she ain't old enough yet—but I guess I know better, deep down. She's old enough. She's pretty enough, too. I guess thet she jest hasn't encouraged them much to this point. Ma Graham remarked 'bout her soon marryin' an' leavin' me. She's right. I've seen the boys tryin' to git her attention in a dozen ways. I always jest thought of it as schoolboy stuff. Not really. One of these days she'll notice 'em too."

"Wish I could see her. S'pose there would be any chance thet she could come out for a while?"

Marty felt a moment of panic. *Ellie come out* here? *The West is full of young men. Why, if she came to see her older sister, she might marry and never return home ag'in!* She fought back her uncomfortable thoughts and responded in an even voice, "Maybe she could come on out on her honeymoon."

"But you said she didn't even have a beau—"

"She don't yet. But, my, thet can happen fast enough. I'm half scared thet she'll have her mind all made up 'bout some young fella by the time thet I git back home."

Missie laughed at her mother's fears. "Now I hardly think that's possible. Not for the short time you'll be away. Are you sure you can stay only for two weeks? Seems like it's hardly worth coming all that way for such a short time."

"We couldn't possibly stay longer. Takes a week to come out an' a week to go home. By the time we git back, we'll have been gone a whole month. It's a busy time of the year, as well. Pa left his boys completely on their own fer the summer hayin' an' all, an' Clare has to git his house ready. Luke is studyin' hard for his college exams an'—"

"Dear little Luke." Missie's voice was gentle. "How is he?"

A softness filled Marty's eyes. "He's not changed. Growed a little, I guess, but he's still got his same ways. Remember how he liked to cuddle up close in your lap when he was a young'un? Well, I git the feelin' sometimes thet he'd still like to do thet—iffen society wouldn't condemn it. He finds other ways to show love now. 'Member how you always used to pick me birthday strawberries? Well, yer pa broke up the pasture where the strawberries grew so well, so the last couple a' years the kids have jest forgot the strawberries. This year Luke decided thet I needed my birthday berries, so he went out real early an' went a-lookin' fer 'em. Had to really work hard, but he came back with a cupful. They was little and a mite on the green side, but I never tasted any better berries—ever."

"An' he's still doing well in school?"

"He's a good student, but he's through at school now. The teacher says thet she's given him everythin' thet she can give. He's read everythin' in sight an' still can't git enough."

"What will he do? He can't just quit."

"He plans to go on. Wants to go to the city fer college. I'm glad—an' scared—an' sad, all at one time. I hate to see him go off alone like thet. Seems so young. He's only fifteen."

"Is he plannin' to be a teacher?"

"A doctor."

"A doctor?" Missie's tone was both surprised and admiring.

"He's had his heart set on it for a number of years now. He's talked to Doc Watkins 'bout it, too. Doc is pleased as a pappy. He doesn't have any children of his own an' he's takin' great pleasure in nursin' Luke's ambitions."

"That would be nice to have a doctor in the family."

"Luke says thet he wants to help people. He's always wanted to help people, an' with so many towns not havin' a doctor—"

"What I wouldn't give to have a doctor here." Missie was wistful. "Young boy of our neighbor's broke his arm last year. There was no one to set it proper-like. He'll always have a twisted, almost useless arm, just because . . ." Missie's words trailed off. "I keep thinkin', *What if it had been Nathan?*"

Marty looked up with troubled eyes. She knew a mother's heart and the panic that one felt when a doctor was nowhere around when one was sorely needed. She too breathed a prayer that somehow this frontier settlement might soon have a doctor, but she also prayed with some reservation. *Not Lukey. Please, not Luke.*

Missie interrupted her thoughts and her silent prayers.

"Tell me about the neighbors. Do we still have the same

people livin' round about?"

"Pretty much. The Coffins moved on back to the area thet they came from. Mrs. Coffin never did really take to our community. Some said thet she jest couldn't stand bein' away from her twin sister. After they lost their little girl—remember the sickly little one?—well, after they lost her, Mrs. Coffin insisted that they go on back to their home. Some new people on their land now. Called the Kentworths. Not friendly folk at all. All the neighbors have tried to git acquainted an' have been told not to bother. People say thet he's a lawbreaker an' jest doesn't want folks snoopin' round. Thet's what he calls it when anyone comes a-visitin'—snoopin' round. She's most as bitter and disagreeable as he is, so fer the time we jest have to sit tight an' pray fer 'em and watch fer a chance to show our carin'. Must be awful to live with such inner bitterness."

Missie nodded her head in agreement.

Marty went on, "Most of the other neighbors are the same as before, I guess. The Grahams are as dear friends as ever. Sally Anne has three girls, 'most growed up now.

"Tommie's Fran jest had a baby boy. He's six years younger than Tom, Jr., the boy who had been the baby fer a good while. Tom is thrilled with the new little fella."

"An' the Marshalls? How are they doin'?"

"It's sad," Marty answered, "sad to see the Marshalls an' their son, but it's beautiful, too. There is so much love there. Rett is a very loving child. He's a young man really, but he is still a child. Wanda and Cam really love 'im. He is so good with animals thet it's 'most uncanny. Wild or tame—they all seem to understand Rett."

"An' Wanda's happy?"

"Happy? Yah, she's happy. She needs to rely on her God daily, though. She has her hard times, but I'm sure thet she wouldn't be tradin' her boy fer all the boys in town."

Missie shook her head as she thought of the grief that Wanda had carried. "She has suffered so much," she said softly.

"Yah," acknowledged Marty, "she has suffered—suffered and growed. Sometimes it seems to take the one to bring the other."

"When one does suffer, it is good to see that it hasn't been wasted—that the sufferer allows God to make it a blessin' rather than a bitterness," Missie expressed.

Marty nodded and then went on. "Wanda and Ma Graham both sent their love. They sent some small gifts to ya, too. We have some packages from them in the trunk. Pa and I decided thet the things we brought with us would jest wait until tomarra. No sense rushin' into everythin' tonight."

"Now that you've mentioned gifts, I'm not sure I can wait 'til mornin'," Missie laughed. "Sorta like teasin' a body—"

"They'll keep. We didn't want to come a-rushin' in here handin' out goodies right an' left. You might have understood, but Nathan and Josiah might be a-thinkin' thet's all grandparents are fer."

Missie laughed. "I'm a-thinkin' my sons have you all sorted out already. They seem to know right off that you're here just to spoil 'em."

"We'll have to be careful, but it sure'd be easy to spoil a bit, all right. Clae's girl, Esther Sue, and Nandry's four shore think thet we are there jest to humor them. 'Course they like attention from their uncles as well. Arnie does most of the fussin'. Arnie really loves young'uns. The others all love the little ones, too, but it is Arnie who never seems to tire of 'em, though he pretends he does."

"An' Joe still hasn't gone off to seminary? Has he changed his mind?"

"Oh, no. He's as set on it as ever. I'm hopin' thet he'll be able to go next year."

"Oh, it's so good to catch up a bit! Makes me feel closer to them somehow. I've missed them all so much."

Marty's eyes filled with tears. "An' we've missed you. Missie, you'll never know how many—" She shook her head and stopped short. "No, I won't say it. I'm here now with you. I see ya have a lovely home, two beautiful boys, thet you're happy. I've told the Lord so many times thet if He'd jest give me this special treat, I'd thank Him with great thankfulness. Now I'm here an' I'm gonna keep my promise. I *am* thankful, Missie— so very thankful." Tears finally spilled down Marty's face, and Missie went to kneel before her and put her arms around her.

"Oh, Mama," she said, "I've longed for you so often. I promised the Lord that I'd be content with seein' you, too. An' here I've been upset because you can't stay longer. I'm ashamed of myself. We'll just make every minute that we have together count. We'll fill our time with so much happiness that we'll have barrels of memories to keep us when the time comes that we need to part again."

Marty smoothed Missie's hair. "Thet sounds like a grand idea," she said. "I've tucked away a few of these precious memories already."

Missie stood up. "Well," she said, "let's just get on with another one. Willie has developed a real liking for popcorn before bed, so let's go pop us some. He says that there just isn't anything better than to have a close family chat over popcorn. It's warm, an' homey, an' fillin'." Missie laughed and led the way to the big kitchen. "I always feel like a little girl sneakin' in where her mama doesn't want her when I do this. Wong is so fussy. But I always clean up real careful-like."

The popcorn was soon ready, and Clark and Willie were called to join them in the living room. The visiting continued, as Willie and Missie asked all about the neighbors, the school, the church. With deep emotion, Willie wanted to know how his pa, Zeke LaHaye, was *really* doing.

"I think thet a trip on out here would do him a world of good," Clark commented. "He needs to get a fresh outlook on things. Oh, he still loves his farm, but yer brother has most taken over now. Zeke loves his grandkids too, but he still misses yer ma somethin' awful. He sent a little parcel with us."

Missie could stand it no longer. "All of this talk of parcels an' presents from back home—an' they plan to make us wait until mornin'! How can a body sleep tonight not knowin' what's in thet there trunk?"

After some laughter and teasing, it was decided that the trunk and its contents would be brought in and enjoyed before retiring, even though the hour was late.

After the trunk was placed in the room and the straps removed, Missie dove in with a will, laying to one side those things intended for the children. She squealed and cried by turn, enjoying every item that had come with love from those "back home."

"We'll have Nandry's raspberry preserves for breakfast," she declared, holding up a sparkling jar.

The hour was late when they finally cleared up the clutter and said good-night.

Marty went to bed with an overflowing heart. Her prayers had been answered—and now she finally felt that she could sleep for a solid week.

Chapter Ten

Busy Days

The next day even Marty was coaxed on horseback in order that she might be given a tour of the ranch. She enjoyed the tiny flowers that nobly bloomed beside the trail; she thrilled to the sight of Willie's herds of cattle feeding on the hillsides; she loved the placid mountains lined up against the sky in the distance. But she did *not* enjoy the wind sweeping across the prairie, pulling at her hair and skirt, nor the miles and miles of seeming emptiness. Missie scarcely could remember the feeling, so she did not notice her mother's silence as her eyes swept the horizon. All Missie saw now was Willie's land as she had grown to love it.

Sunday arrived and with it some visitors to the LaHaye spread. At two o'clock in the afternoon, the opening hymn of their regular Sunday service was led by Henry. Clark and Marty had been happy to renew their acquaintance with the wagon driver. Henry had changed much in those few short years. No longer a bashful, hesitant boy, instead he was a sincere and confident man, presenting an attractive wife and a two-year-old son, Caldwell. Henry's pride shone in his eyes.

As they sang the hymn, Marty glanced around her. Some of the cowhands were there. She couldn't remember all the names, though she had been introduced. There was Cookie— she had no problem remembering Cookie—and Rusty and Lane. The other two she could not remember. Another neighborhood family had joined them for the service. Marty saw the small boy with the twisted arm, and her heart went out to him. These were the Newtons, a young couple with four young sons. Juan and Maria and their baby girl and young son were not in attendance this time. Missie kept an eye on the road that twisted down the hill, hoping that they would arrive, but when the service had ended they still hadn't come. Missie was worried. It was the second Sunday in a row that the De la Rosas had not showed up. They were not away from home; Scottie had seen them Friday. No one was ill, for they had all been in town together. Missie could not think of a reason for their absence. They had been so regular in attendance. She must call on them and see if there was some problem.

After the singing, Willie led the service and Clark was asked, as honored guest, to give the Bible lesson. The people were attentive, and Marty even heard an occasional quiet "Amen."

After the service had ended, Missie served coffee and some of Wong's delicious doughnuts. They sat and visited, sharing their daily experiences and joys. Marty and Clark were glad for the opportunity to get to know some of Missie and Willie's neighbors. They all seemed to feel that the service was a special time in their week.

The cowboys were the first to take their reluctant leave. It was time for their shift; Scottie would be watching for them.

Next the Newtons also left. Mr. Newton as yet did not employ many hands on his spread and needed to get back in the saddle himself. He stated that they hadn't been bothered much with rustlers lately, but one could never tell when they might decide to strike. The small, defenseless ranches were easy picking. The Newtons promised to be back again the next Sunday.

The Henry Kleins stayed for supper. Wong was happy for the chance to show off his culinary skills. Nathan and Josiah, glad for a playmate, took Caldwell out to the patio to play with a delighted Max, who ran around in circles with excited yelps to remind them that for the last few days he had been getting very little attention.

Marty chatted with Melinda Klein while Missie fussed about the table, setting it with the good dishes and making sure that everything looked its best. Marty soon came to feel very close to this young woman. They had shared similar experiences in their introduction to the West, both having lost a young husband in tragic accidents. Marty was glad that Melinda had Henry to help her over the hurt and confusion of losing the one she loved, while so far away from friends and family. *And I'm glad I had Clark*, she thought with a quick glance at him across the room.

Henry, too, was anxious for news from the home area. Though Clark and Marty knew few of the people that Henry would have claimed as neighbors, they were able to tell him some of the general news from the district.

Soon after the evening meal, the Kleins left for home and the boys were tucked in for the night. After their double portion of bedtime stories, they settled down, not to be heard from again till morning. Missie declared that the excitement of Sundays always tired them out.

Marty too felt tired, even though she had gradually been catching up on her sleep. Willie informed her that it was the change in the altitude. Marty was willing to accept any excuse for her laziness. All she knew was that she was longing for her bed.

She hid a yawn and tried to get back into the conversation. Clark and Willie were making plans for the morning. It sounded like wherever they were going, it would be a long ride. Willie was asking Missie if she wished to go. Marty was already stiff from her short ride of the day before. She wasn't sure that she could handle another horseback ride, but Missie was answering, "I thought Mama an' I should go on over to see Maria. I can't understand why they have missed two Sundays.

If it's okay with Mama, we'll go an' see what we can find out. I'm anxious for Mama an' Maria to meet. You'll never believe Maria," Missie said, turning to Marty. "She speaks very good English now. Me—I hardly got a decent start on Spanish."

So it will be the saddle again tomorrow. Marty winced at the thought. Not only would she ride tomorrow, but from what she had understood, she would ride a long way. The De la Rosas were not *near* neighbors.

Marty nodded her head in agreement, hoping that Missie did not read the hesitation in her eyes.

Missie continued, "We should leave by nine. I think that we'd better take the team so Mama won't need to ride so soon again, not bein' used to it. 'Sides, it's a fair ways an' we'll need to take the boys. Could you have Scottie see that the team is ready for us, please?"

Willie nodded and Marty sighed in relief. Everyone, now having settled on the plans for the morrow, decided that sleep would be needed to carry them through. They bade each other good-night and headed for their beds.

Chapter Eleven

Marty Meets Maria

The sun rose over the distant hills early the next morning and right from the sunrise seemed to pour forth angry heat.

Around nine, Willie brought the team around, and Missie loaded her canteens and her sons. Marty placed her bonnet firmly on her head as protection from the sun and wished for a cooler gown.

"My, it be warm!" she exclaimed, but Missie did not seem to be bothered by the warm day.

"A breeze should come up an' cool things off some," she responded, clucked to the team and they were off.

They had not gone far before Marty could feel the breeze, though she might have been tempted to refer to it as a gale. It was not cooling. In fact, Marty felt that the wind was even hotter than the sun. It whipped at her cheeks, drying and warming them. It tore at her skirts and made the brim of her bonnet flap in agitation. Marty did not care for wind, and she wished that the one which was blowing now would blow elsewhere. "I guess I've gotten used to the wind," Missie remarked as Marty tried to hold her bonnet down with one hand and her skirts with the other.

Nathan and Josiah rode comfortably on the first part of the journey; then began the persistent question, "How much longer?" Missie dealt with it good-naturedly until Nathan began to tease his younger brother for lack of something else to do, and then she stopped the horses and lifted the youngsters down for a break. They were each given a drink from a canteen and a couple of cookies and instructed to play in the shade of the wagon while the ladies stretched their limbs in a short walk. There was no shade for walking, so there was no temptation to linger. In fact, Marty was glad to be back in the wagon and moving again.

When they came to the river, Marty glanced up and down its length for a bridge. There was none. Missie confidently headed the horses into the stream, explaining as she did so that it used to flow deeper at that point until the men of the area widened the riverbed some and allowed the stream to spread out. "Now," said Missie, "it's safe to cross here most any time of year."

Marty, relieved to hear that it was safe, still gripped the wagon seat with white knuckles until they climbed the bank on the other side.

Crossing the river was the most exciting part of the journey for the boys. Marty heard them squeal with delight as the swirling water foamed about the wagon wheels. Once across, they began to coax their mother to hurry the team and complained that they were too crowded, too hot and too hungry.

Missie eventually handed the reins to Marty and took Josiah on her lap. Without Josiah to torment, Nathan too became quiet.

It was almost noon before the De la Rosas' buildings came into view. Marty saw a large, low ranchhouse, built of the same stone as Missie's home though not quite as spacious. It nestled among brown hills, and there was not even a spring to add greenness to the area. Missie informed Marty that the De la Rosas were fortunate in having all the water they needed from the deep well they had dug. The well now was showing its worth as a windmill turned busily in the ever-present wind, causing a pump to send a constant stream of water from its spout into a large animal trough.

"Well, it's nice to know thet the wind is good fer some-thin'," muttered Marty under her breath as she guided the team into the yard and directed them to the hitching rail.

A young woman came rushing from the house.

"Missie!" she cried. "Oh, I'm so glad you have come. I've been missing our visits!" She saw Marty and stopped with embarrassment. "Oh, please do excuse my bad manners. I did not know that Missie was not alone. You must be the mother. The one that Missie has missed and cried and prayed for."

Marty nodded.

"And I am Maria—the mindless one," she joked. "I run heedless when I see a friend."

Marty laughed and extended her hand, then changed her mind and hugged Maria close.

"Missie has told me of ya. Yer such a special friend, and I am so glad to meet ya," Marty said warmly.

"And I you," said Maria, giving Marty a warm embrace in return, "though I must say that seeing you makes me even more longing for the mama of my own. It has been so long . . ."

Maria did not finish her sentence. Missie had lifted the boys down and they were clamoring for some attention.

"Where's José?" asked Nathan.

"He's in the house, where we all should be out of this hot sun. Come, you must get in out of the heat. You are brave to come on such a day." And Maria hastened them all into her home.

"José is in the kitchen bothering the cook," she told Nathan. "You may get him and you can play in his room. I don't think that even our patient Carlos could put up with *two* small boys in the kitchen."

Nathan went to find José, and the ladies walked into the coolness of the sitting room, Josiah in tow. Marty felt so much better out of the sun. She slipped off her bonnet and was glad to wipe the perspiration from her face with a handkerchief. *My, it was a hot trip!*

Maria seated them and went for cool drinks. Upon hearing the two older boys chattering as they came from the kitchen, Josiah decided to tag along with them to José's room.

The ladies were left to sip cold tea and visit. The talk was centered around the family, area news and ranching. Marty was included, though some of the phrases that the girls used regarding ranching were new to her.

"You should have waited for a day more less hot," said Maria and then laughed at her mixed-up English. "How you say it?" she asked Missie.

"A cooler day."

"My goodness—cooler, no! There is nothing cool about this day. How can it be more cool than something that is not cool at all?"

Marty and Missie laughed at Maria's reasoning. It seemed to make sense.

"Anyway," said Maria, "it is very warm to be in the sun. We are used to it here, but you, Mrs. Davis, must find it bad to you."

"It is warm," admitted Marty.

"Well, I guess we should have waited. But who knows, it might get hotter instead of cooler, an' I did want to see you, Maria."

"A special reason?" asked Maria seriously.

"Rather special. We've been missin' you on Sundays, an' I was afraid—well, I wondered—that is, I hoped nothin' was wrong."

At the mention of the Sunday service, Maria's head drooped.

"I wanted to go. I missed it. But Juan—well, he is not sure. Not sure that we do the right thing. At home we teach our boy one thing—one way to pray, one way to worship God—and at the meeting, you teach him another way. It puzzles him. You understand? Juan, he thinks that we should not confuse our son with more than one God."

"But, Maria," exclaimed Missie, "we've talked about that! It's the same God. We worship the same God, just in a little different way."

"I know, I know," said Maria, her hands fluttering expressively. "I know all that. And I think that Juan, he even understands that. But he is frightened—frightened that José will not understand and he will not wish to worship God at all. Do you not see?"

"Yes, I see," said Missie slowly, tears filling her eyes. "I see."

"Oh, I am so glad. So glad that you understand. I was so afraid that you would not be able to see how we felt. I did not want you to think ill of me."

"Maria, I would never think ill of you."

Maria turned to hide her own tears. For a moment she couldn't speak, and then she turned back to her guests and the tears were running down her cheeks.

"You must pray for us. Right now Juan has many doubts, many questions. He cannot leave the church of his past, but he has here no church of his own. He does not want his child to grow up without the proper church teaching, but he is no longer sure what he wants him taught. There was much about Juan's church that he did not agree with, but he loved his church. He has not forsaken it. He will never forsake it. In the services at your house we have heard new and strange things from the Bible. We did not know of them before. It takes much wisdom, much time, much searching of the heart to know the truth. Please be patient with us, Missie. And please pray for us that we may know the truth. One day we think, 'This is it,' and the next day we say, 'No, that is it.' It is hard—so very hard."

"I understand," said Missie. "We will pray. We will pray that you will find the truth—not that you will believe as we believe, but that you will find the truth. We believe with all of our heart that God has given His truth to us in His Son Jesus Christ, that He came to die for us and to forgive us our sins, and—" Missie stopped short. "But you believe that too, Maria. You have told me that Jesus is the only way that one can come to God."

"Oh, yes," said Maria. "That is the truth."

"Then all that we really need to pray about is that God will show you and Juan if it's all right to worship with us."

"I . . . I guess so. We have been taught one way—you another."

"We will continue to pray."

"It is so important to Juan to raise his children in the correct way. You see, his family—" But Maria stopped midsentence and hastened to her feet. "I must see if Carlos has our coffee and cakes ready. You will have cooled enough by now to be able to enjoy some of Carlos' coffee." She hurried away without waiting for a reply.

The talk over the coffee turned to lighter matters. They chatted about new material, dress patterns, and the gardens that were growing daily in spite of the heat. Missie finally announced that they must go, and Maria sent José and Nathan to find Pedro, the yard hand, to bring the team and hitch up the wagon.

While the boys were running off to find the old man and give him the message, the ladies prepared to leave.

"Please," said Maria, "please could we have a prayer together? I have missed it so."

They knelt to pray. Missie prayed first, followed by Marty, and then it was Maria's turn. She began slowly, in carefully chosen English; and then she stopped and turned to the other two ladies. "Do you mind—will you excuse me—if I talk to God in my own language? I know He understands my heart in any language, but I think that He understands *my* tongue better in the language of my birth." At their nods and smiles, Maria continued her prayer. Never had Marty heard a more fervent one. Maria poured out her soul to her God in honeyflowing Spanish. Though Marty could not understand a word of it, she understood the spirit of the prayer and her heart prayed along with Maria. Surely God would answer this young woman's yearning for the truth.

Chapter Twelve

The Rescue

The weather turned a little cooler, though still too warm for Marty's liking; but at least it was bearable. Missie and Marty kept quite close to the shelter of the house, but Clark rode with the men almost daily. His farmer's heart responded to the wide expanse of hillsides and roaming cattle, and he declared many times his love of the mountains.

Nathan clamored for his fair share of his grandfather's attention. He was anxious to show what he considered his part of the ranch to Clark. As yet, he was not allowed to roam freely on the open range. There were well-worn trails closer to home that he claimed as his own. He had ridden them since he had been a baby carried on his mother's back. Now Josiah had replaced Nathan on Missie's horse, and Nathan was allowed the pleasure of his own pony.

"Could ya ride with me today, Grandpa?" Nathan begged at the breakfast table.

"Well, I shore don't see why not," answered Clark. "I 'spect maybe yer pa will be able to git by without me fer this here one day."

Nathan took his grandfather's words seriously; "Ya can help him again tomarra," he assured Clark, causing laughter to ripple around the table.

"An' where do we be ridin' today?"

"I'll show ya the west ridge."

"An' are there lots of excitin' things to see on the west ridge?"

Nathan nodded his head vigorously, his mouth was too full of scrambled eggs to speak.

"Well, then," said Clark, "why don't we jest go on out fer a look-see?"

Nathan's eyes twinkled in anticipation. He hurried through his meal and bounced down from the table without asking to be excused.

"What horse shall I tell Scottie to saddle for ya, Grandpa?"

"Nathan," said Willie quietly, indicating Nathan's empty chair.

Nathan crawled back up reluctantly and looked over at his mother, then back at his father. "May I be excused, sir?" he asked, subdued.

Willie nodded and Nathan swung down from the chair.

"What horse—" he began, but Clark stopped him with a laugh.

"I think thet Scottie be busy enough without worryin' none 'bout me. I'll saddle ol' Turk when I git down there."

Nathan spun around and was gone. "I'll get Spider," he called over his shoulder as he ran out of the door, then followed it with, "Too bad Joey's too little."

"Joey?" questioned Marty.

Missie laughed. "I thought and thought of a name for my second son that wouldn't be all chopped up in a nickname. I thought that I had one, too. Josiah. Surely no one could shorten that. But I wasn't counting on Nathan. He's called him Joey since the day he arrived."

"I think it's rather nice," Marty mused.

"Well, I guess it's all right—You know what I've decided? I've decided that 'most any name is all right as long as it's spoken with love."

Marty agreed.

Clark finished his coffee and turned to Willie. "Well, cowboy, it looks like you'll jest have to do yer best to be a-wranglin' without me today. I've got me another pardner."

Willie grinned. "Wish I could come with ya, but I promised Hugh Caly thet I'd ride on over and take a look at some new stock he brought in. Yer lucky to be a-missin' thet ride. It's a long, hot one, an' to save some miles we pass right through some bad cactus territory. Near scratches the clothes right off ya."

"Thet there west ridge sounds better 'n better to me," Clark smiled.

"Nothing much of danger on the west ridge. Thet's why we allow Nathan to ride there. Pretty lifeless over there. Ya'll be lucky to even spy a rattler slitherin' off."

"Well, iffen there be a rattler, I do hope that it slithers off, all right," said Clark. "I still haven't grown overfond of 'em."

"Jest don't surprise 'em," said Willie, "an' you'll be all right."

When Clark reached the barn, Scottie was unobtrusively giving Nathan a hand with the saddling of Spider. Clark went into the corral to bring out Turk. He still wasn't too good with a rope, but he managed to get the horse on the second try.

They saddled up and left the yard, Missie calling to them as they rode out to make sure they both had full canteens.

"Ma always worries," confided Nathan in a whisper, to which Clark responded, "Thet's what mas be for."

They rode to the west, then turned toward the south and followed the ridge for a few miles. There really wasn't much to see but an occasional glimpse at part of the mountain chain as they topped one of the higher hills. Often they could look out to the east and see cattle, as Willie's herd fed its way across the prairie. Once or twice, they spotted a cowboy as he hazed the cattle. The sun was high in the sky when Clark suggested that they pull over in the shelter of some big rocks and eat the lunch Missie had sent along. Nathan seemed to like the idea. The eating time was the most important part of any trail ride. Nathan crawled down from Spider and ground-tied him. Clark did likewise with Turk, looking around cautiously to make sure there were no rattlers sharing the rocks with them. He noticed Nathan do likewise.

"If rattlers are here, Grandpa, they'll be in the sun 'stead of on this shady side," he said. "But still Pa says ya always got to check to be sure."

Clark was pleased with the boy's knowledge of his environment and his carefulness.

"How much further we goin'?" asked Clark, as they munched their sandwiches.

"Not much, I guess. Nothin' to see down there 'cept some ol' hills with holes in 'em."

"Ol' hills with holes?"

Nathan nodded.

"What kind of holes?"

"Pa says they used to mine it."

"Mine it?"

"Yeah."

"What kind of mine?"

"Dunno. Pa says fer me to stay away from the holes. He says thet they are dang'rous. Some stuff is gittin' rotten or somethin'."

"Best we stay away from 'em then," agreed Clark, but he planned on asking Willie about the old mines when he got home.

They had just finished their lunch and were gathering things together when they heard an approaching horse. The rider was coming full gallop and Clark stood up to see what the reason might be. One did not usually ride at such pace in the heat of the midday sun.

A young rider approached them, his legs beating at the sides of his horse and his unruly hair flying in the wind. Clark could hear him shout now and then, but he couldn't understand a word he was saying.

"Who's thet?" Clark asked the young Nathan.

For a moment Nathan just stood and stared without answering.

"Who is he? Ya know?" Clark asked again.

Nathan roused then, shaking his head.

The rider pounded closer, and Clark could plainly hear him sobbing now. Clark stepped forward to be ready to stop the horse when the boy drew near.

"You gotta come!" the frantic boy screamed even before he reached them. "You gotta come quick! Andy and Abe, they—"

He had reached them, and Clark hauled in the lathered horse.

"Whoa there," he said, reaching up in one smooth movement both to pull the horse to a halt and to run a quieting hand over its neck.

"You gotta come—" the boy's voice was agitated and hoarse with emotion.

Clark moved a hand to the boy. "Jest take it easy. Take it easy. We'll come. Now ya calm down some 'n' tell—"

"Abe an' Andy!" cried the boy, tears making tracks down his dust-covered cheeks. "Abe an' Andy are in there."

"Take it easy," Clark said again. "Jest tell it slow-like."

"We gotta hurry!" the boy barked impatiently.

"We'll hurry," said Clark. "But first we gotta know where to hurry to."

"The mine. The ol' mine shaft—they're in there. It fell on 'em. They'll never git out."

"Where?"

"Over there. We were lookin' 'em over an' the timbers broke an' the mine fell in—"

But Clark was already gathering the reins of his horse. "Nathan," he said, "can ya ride home alone? Does yer pa ever let ya do thet?"

"Sure," said Nathan, his eyes wide.

"Look, son," said Clark, pulling the boy close. "I want ya to ride on back to the ranch. Tell Scottie, or whoever is around, thet some kids are trapped in a mine. Tell 'em to bring shovels an' a wagon an' come on the double. Ya got thet?"

Nathan nodded his head in agreement, his eyes wide with fright.

"Now ya ride on home. Take yer time—do ya hear? Don't

try to go fast. Jest take yer time an' be careful. I'm gonna go with this here boy an' help those kids. All right?"

Clark boosted Nathan onto his pony and watched as the small boy headed back to the ranch on the familiar path. He was not concerned about the boy becoming lost. Nathan knew the way well. Clark was worried that panic might cause him to travel too fast and maybe end up in a spill. Nathan turned once to look back at his grandfather. "Remember. Go slow," Clark called to him, and the boy waved his hand.

The sobbing of the boy beside him brought Clark's head around.

"Okay, son. You lead the way. Take it easy. A fall with yer horse won't help yer friends none."

They started for the mine, the boy's spent horse wheezing for breath in choking gasps. Clark found that the mine was farther away than he had hoped.

The boy still cried sporadically. He pushed his horse as fast as the poor creature could go. When they finally reached an opening in the side of a hill, he threw himself off.

"They're in there!" he cried. "We gotta git 'em out."

Smoke-colored dust still lingered in the air, and Clark could easily see that recently there had been a cave-in.

"You know this mine?" he asked the boy.

"Some," the boy admitted with downcast eyes, and Clark could see that he knew it was forbidden territory.

Some boards that obviously had closed off the cave entrance had been pried off and discarded at the side of its open mouth.

"Tell me 'bout it," Clark said, and as the boy hesitated, Clark took his arm. "Yer friends are in there. Remember? Now I don't know one thing about thet there cave. Tell me 'bout it. Does it have more than one branch? How far back were ya? Did the timbers collapse more'n once?"

The boy responded. "It has three main tunnels. The first one takes off real quick to the right. It's a short one. Don't think thet the miners found anything there, so they jest left it. The second one goes off to the right, too. But the fellas are in the left one. It's the biggest an' was used the most. The timbers are really bad in there. The shaft goes down deeper in the left one. Sometimes the steps are real steep an' slippery. We was climbin' up an' we kept slippin', so we grabbed hold of the side timbers to pull ourselves, an' thet's when it . . ." He couldn't continue but put his face in his hands and sobbed.

Clark stayed long enough to hold him for a moment. "It's okay. We'll git 'em. Are there any shovels?"

The boy shook his head. "We can use our hands," he snuffled.

"Yer not comin' back in," said Clark, seeing the terror in the boy's face.

"But I gotta," he said through sobs. "I gotta."

"No, yer needed here. They're gonna come from the ranch. Ya need to tell 'em where to go. They'll have shovels. Ya tell 'em too 'bout those rotten timbers. Ya hear?"

The boy nodded. Clark hoped that he would be able to wait calmly without further panic.

Clark gently pushed the young boy to a sitting position on a nearby rock. "Ya jest stay right there an' wait fer those men. Now, it might seem a long time 'til they be comin', but they'll be here. Ya jest keep watchin' fer 'em an' wave 'em on over here. Ya okay now?"

The boy nodded again, affirming that he was. His face was still white beneath the smears of dust and tears.

Clark turned and headed for the mine. The door was low and he had to stoop to enter. Old beams above his head appeared as his eyes adjusted to the dimness. The supports looked fairly stable in some places and sagging and broken in others. Clark moved away from the light at the entrance and felt his way along the passage. He had not gone far when he found the first tunnel off to the right just as the boy had described. He continued on, feeling his way with his hands and his feet. A low-hanging beam caught him by surprise and he banged his head against the knotted lumber. For a minute he felt dizzy with the pain, but he steadied himself until he had his bearings. From then on he went forward with one arm outstretched above his head.

Clark ducked his way past other obstructions. How he

wished for a light. He figured the boys must have used some kind of torches or lanterns to find their way around. Clark discovered the second right-hand tunnel. *Only one more to go,* he told himself. The tunnel should soon swing to the left. After several yards of total darkness, Clark felt the tunnel veer sharply. The smell of dust was heavy in the air now. Clark was forced to stop and tie his handkerchief over his nose. He started down the left fork and soon came to one of the boy's steep places. Catching Clark off guard, before he knew what was happening his feet had slipped out from under him, and he felt himself sliding downward on his back. The rocks cut into him, scraping away shirt and skin. After he had come to a halt and felt cautiously about, Clark regained his feet and pressed slowly forward, testing carefully with his foot before he put his weight on it. Again and again the tunnel took a downward turn, but Clark was ready for them, most only a step or two. And then, just ahead of him, Clark thought he heard a groan. He fell to his hands and knees and felt his way forward.

"Hello," he called. "Hello. Do you hear me? Hello."

Another groan answered him and Clark crawled on.

Soon he was in contact with a slight body. "Do you hear me?" he asked, reaching for the boy's wrist and the pulse. The boy stirred. Clark felt a faint pulsebeat and breathed a prayer of thanks.

"Son," he asked anxiously, "Son. Can you hear me? Are ya awake?"

In answer the boy began to cry. "Ya came," he sobbed. "Ya came."

"It's all right." Clark soothed him, brushing the dirt and debris from around his head and brushing his hair back out of his face. "It's all right. Where are ya hurt? Can ya get up."

"My leg," sobbed the boy. "My leg is caught under thet beam."

"We'll git it out. We'll have it out in no time. Ya jest hang in there."

"Abe," said the boy. "Did ya git Abe yet?"

"Not yet," answered Clark.

Clark began to feel around in the darkness. He had to discover just what was holding the boy's leg. He found the beam, a big piece of timber, too thick and too long for him to be able to tackle without some kind of tool.

He went on searching, feeling around for the other boy. Carefully he made his way over the rubble and back again, the sharp stones cutting into the flesh of his palms. Nothing. He crawled on. He nearly missed it; but, just as his hand slid over some rocky debris, he felt something soft to the touch. It was a boot. Clark allowed his hand to search out the area. The boy was almost totally buried under the cave-in. Clark began to dig away at the rock and dirt, trying not to dislodge any more of the tunnel wall in his haste.

At length he brought forth an arm. He dug on, frantically searching out the place where the head might be, eventually uncovering it. He longed for a light. If only he could see to discover the condition of the boy. His hands traced over the temple, the face, the back of the head and back again. They told him all that he needed to know. Clark crawled back to Andy.

"Andy," he said. "Andy. Ya still with me, boy?"

The boy groaned his answer.

"Andy, I've gotta try to git yer leg out. Now, I can't move thet there beam. It's too big an' heavy an' I don't have anything to cut it with. I'm gonna have to try to dig out from under yer leg and git it out thet way. It's gonna hurt, Andy. Can ya take it?"

Andy was crying again. "Yah," he said. "We gotta git out. These timbers keep creakin' like they're gonna break ag'in."

Clark crawled around, feeling for a sharp rock. He found one that he thought would make a tool of sorts and began to dig around the boy's leg. At first he worked far enough away from the boy that the digging did not bother him, but as the rubble was gradually cleared away, the leg began to shift and the boy moaned in pain. This turned into a tortured scream, but Clark dug on, trying his hardest to be as gentle as he knew how. He must get him out, and quickly, for the boy was right: Clark, too, could hear the timbers snapping and creaking and feared that, at any time, they might give way and pour forth more rocks and earth.

It seemed forever to Clark until he had a hole clawed away beneath Andy's foot deep enough to coax the boy's ankle out.

He would have to slip off the boot in order to make the foot squeeze under. Pulling off the boot from the broken foot made Andy scream again in pain. Clark almost succumbed to the cries and stopped twisting, but he knew that he would be signing the boy's life away if he did. He had dug away the earth to sheer rock. He could make the opening no bigger for the injured ankle to pass through. If Andy was to be freed, he must pull him loose now. Clark gritted his teeth, took the foot as gently as he could, and forced the injured leg out from under the beam. Mercifully, Andy fainted. Clark wiped dirt from the boy's face and loosened his collar. Then he picked him up gently and started carefully back up the tunnel.

Stumbling along in the darkness, feeling his way with an outstretched toe, bumping against rocks and beams that obstructed the path was treacherous going. The steep steps upward were the most difficult. One time he had to slide the boy up ahead of him, then claw his way up behind him and go on again. On and on he stumbled and fought until at least he could sense, more than see, the tunnel to his right. He breathed a thanksgiving prayer and hurried on. The tunnel floor was smoother now and walking was easier. Soon Clark passed the second tunnel as well. If only the men from the ranch would be there with a light and some shovels.

And then, just ahead, Clark saw the opening of the mine. He hastened forward and burst out to fresh air and glaring sunshine. The boy was sitting in the shade on the same rock where Clark had seated him. He sprang to his feet when Clark made an appearance.

"Ya found Andy!" he cried. "Andy. Andy, ya okay?" He was crying again. "Is he dead, mister?"

"Naw," said Clark. "He's okay. He's got a busted foot, but he'll be okay. Run over there to my saddle an' git thet there canteen. He needs a drink." The boy ran away in a flash.

Clark laid the boy gently on the ground in the shade. He stood to full height and looked off in the direction of the ranch. In the distance he could see whirls of dust. They were on their way. He couldn't wait. The timbers might give way at any moment and then the other boy, Abe, would be buried deep within the mine shaft.

He turned to the boy who was kneeling beside his friend Andy, trying to help him with a few swallows of water.

"Listen," he said. "They are on their way here now. See thet dust over there? It's gonna take 'em awhile to git here. I want ya to take good care of Andy 'til they come, an' when they git here you just tell 'em to wait out here fer me. Ya understand? I know where Abe is, an' I'm gonna go git 'im."

The boy nodded his head and Clark turned and hurried back into the old mine. Traveling more quickly this time with a better idea of what was ahead of him, he still protected himself with a raised arm and a groping foot. But he moved with less caution because he knew that time was a major factor.

As he felt and slipped his way down the left tunnel, he prayed that he might get to Abe before the whole mine collapsed. The dust still hung heavily in the air, but Clark didn't think it was any worse than before. It appeared that there had been no further cave-ins.

He came to the last steep slide and let himself down carefully, trying hard not to disturb any more of the rock around him. At the bottom, he dropped on all fours and felt his way forward to where he had left Abe. In the darkness he found the outstretched arm and the near-buried face, and he began to dig methodically, painstakingly, lifting away the debris from around him. It was slow work. Some of the rocks that buried the boy were boulder-sized, and it took all of Clark's strength to move them to the side. He clawed and pushed, pulled and scratched, tore and pried until at last he had the boy freed from his prison.

He stopped for only a minute to catch his breath, and then he lifted the boy tenderly and once again began the climb to the outside world. Just as he pushed Abe ahead of him up the steep slope, there was a terrifying crack and a monstrous roar, and the ceiling of the cavern collapsed all around him. Pain seared through Clark as a heavy timber fell with sickening impact upon his leg, and then merciful blackness.

Chapter Thirteen

A Double Tragedy

The men in the wagon had just pulled up and begun to throw questions at the boy when the roar from within the cave burst upon them. Another cave-in! The boy crumpled to the ground with a cry of despair; and Andy, who lay on the ground shivering in shock, began to whimper.

"Someone look after thet boy," barked Scottie, and Lane moved forward to examine the youngster and ordered some blankets brought from the wagon.

Willie headed for the mine entrance and was stopped by Scottie's hands.

"I'm goin' in," said Willie.

"No, ya ain't. Nobody's goin' in there 'til we know thet it's finished fallin'."

Willie hesitated and stood listening to the rumbling inside the hillside.

The dust began to sift out of the entrance as they stood and stared, straining their ears. Willie turned to the sobbing boy.

"Did the man who came with ya go in there, boy?"

The boy nodded his head.

"Has he been out a'tall?"

"He brought Andy out."

"Where is he now?"

"He went back in fer Abe."

It was exactly as Willie knew that it would be, yet somehow he had dared to hope that it might not be so.

The rumbling gradually stopped. Willie headed for the wagon and came back with a lantern and a rope. Again Scottie stepped forward and without a word took the lantern from him and lit it.

"Lane," Scottie instructed, "grab these shovels an' follow me."

Willie moved to fall in line.

"Mr. LaHaye," said Scottie, "you ain't goin' in there."

"What ya talkin'—" Willie began, but Scottie interrupted.

"I'm talkin' 'bout you," said Scottie firmly. "You an' yer missus an' those two little boys."

"But—"

"No buts. Thet there mine might *give* ag'in. Ya know thet, an' I know thet."

Scottie then turned to Lane. "I'm not askin' any man to take chances," he said. "You stay several feet behind me an' iffen ya hear a rumble, then run fer it. Now, boy, where do we find 'em?"

The young boy moved forward and was able to again intelligently give the men directions, and then Scottie and Lane moved through the mine opening.

Willie fidgeted at the entry. He wanted to go in and help with the search for Clark. He *would* go in. And then he thought of Missie. Of Missie and his two sons. If anything should happen to her father, she would need her husband even more.

He paced back and forth before the mouth of the mine and then went over to see if there was anything he could do for the young boy who lay groaning on the ground.

He turned to the boy who leaned against the rock outcropping, staring at the gaping hole that had caused all of their misery.

"Boy," he said, "do ya live 'round here?"

"In town," he answered.

"This yer brother?" asked Willie, indicating Andy on the ground.

"My friend. My brother—he's still in there."

"Yer folks be worryin'?"

"I reckon."

"Do ya think thet ya should ride on home an' tell 'em? Yer pa might want to git on over here an' help git yer brother out."

The boy looked surprised that he hadn't thought of that.

"Yah," he said and headed for his grazing horse.

"An' git word to the folks of this here boy too, will ya, son? They can come over and see what they can do to make 'im more comfortable."

The boy cast a backward glance at his friend and hurried off.

From then on there was nothing for Willie to do except watch the entrance of the mine and pray that there would be no more cave-ins. Occasionally he talked to the half-conscious boy or gave him sips of water. The broken foot was painful, but as Willie examined it with his eyes, not wanting to move it, he thought that it looked like it might heal properly. He could see no protruding bones or broken skin.

There was nothing to speed up the minutes as Willie waited. Time after time he started down the mine tunnel, only to think of Scottie's words and turn back.

After what seemed like an eternity, another wagon pulled up. A man whom Willie had seen only once before jumped to the ground before the wagon even stopped rolling. He stopped briefly to touch the face of Andy, give a brief nod to Willie, and then he ran into the entrance of the mine. He did not even carry a lantern.

A woman approached more slowly. Already her face was tear-streaked and her eyes swollen from weeping.

"Is this yer son?" asked Willie with concern in his voice.

The woman knelt beside the boy and smoothed his hair with her hand and wiped the dust from his face with an edge of her simple gown.

"No," she said, her voice trembling. "It's my boy still in there."

"I'm sorry," said Willie.

"We've told 'em—over an' over we've warned 'em. 'Don't go near those mines,' we've said. 'They're not safe.' But bein' boys they jest gotta find out fer themselves." She was sobbing softly, not bothering with the tears that ran down her cheeks.

"Somebody should do something 'bout those caves," the woman went on. "Ya never know whose child might be next."

Willie thought of his own two boys. "We'll git a permit to dynamite 'em, ma'am, jest as soon as we git these folks out."

The boy stirred and the woman spoke to him. "It's okay, Andy. Casey has gone fer yer ma an' pa. They should be here anytime now. They'll git ya on home an' look to thet foot."

Andy, relieved, closed his eyes again.

Willie scanned the hills again and could see another wagon approaching in the distance. It was not long until Andy's folks arrived and the mother was running to him with shrieks and cries. Willie feared that she was going to have hysterics, but her husband calmed her. She fell on the ground beside her son and alternated between scoldings and endearments. The man knelt over the foot and began to prod the ankle. The boy cried out in pain, and the father grimaced and then went about preparing a makeshift cast. It was not a pleasant task. The boy screamed again and again as the foot was straightened and bound. Everyone present had broken into a cold sweat before the ordeal was over. At length the father's gruesome task was done and he buried his face in his hands and sobbed. And still there was no sign of life from the mouth of the mine.

"How long they been in there?" asked one of the mothers.

"I've long since lost track of time," answered Willie. "Seems forever. At least there's been no more rumbles. Thet's a good sign."

He paced back and forth and again ventured into the cave a short distance; and then he heard the scraping and sliding of scuffling feet, and as he strained forward he could see the faint light of a lantern reflecting off the tunnel wall.

He pushed forward more eagerly and soon was face to face with Scottie. Scottie carried the front end of a makeshift stretcher made from broken timbers and Lane stumbled along behind carrying the other end. On the stretcher lay Clark. His face was deathly white and blood-smeared, and the arm that dangled at his side swung lifelessly back and forth.

"Oh, dear God," prayed Willie, and then to the men, "Is he dead?"

Scottie did not answer. Lane finally dared to voice a quiet, "Not quite."

Willie took the lantern that swung from one corner of the stretcher and led the way. As he turned to check on the progress of the men behind him, he noticed the third man. It was the boy's father, and he too bore a burden. In his arms he carried his boy. Willie's eyes asked the question, and this time Scottie answered. "No," was all he said.

Chapter Fourteen

A Day of a Million Years

They took Clark to the ranch on a makeshift bed in the wagon. Even in his unconscious state, he groaned occasionally. They tried to drive as carefully as they could, but the jarring vehicle was distressful at best and a torment at its worst.

Scottie guided the team, turning this way and that as he snaked a pathway home, trying his best to miss chuckholes and bumps. Willie sat with Clark, steadying him and bathing his face with water from the canteen. Except for the lump on his head from the falling beam and the badly injured leg, Clark seemed to have no other wounds. Willie dared to hope that the head injury would be a mild concussion and that Clark would not suffer any serious effects from it.

The leg was another matter. As Willie looked at the severely broken leg with the bone splinter projecting from the skin, he shuddered. How could such a leg heal without the help of a doctor? "Oh, dear God," prayed Willie, "please show us what to do."

As the wagon neared the ranch, an anxious Marty and

Missie hurried out into the yard. Willie chided himself for not thinking to go ahead and prepare his womenfolk, and he jumped from the slow-moving wagon and asked Lane to watch Clark, and Scottie to drive as slowly as he knew how. Then Willie quickened his stride and reached the women slightly ahead of the wagon.

"Clark been hurt?" gasped Marty.

Willie nodded.

"Bad?" cried Missie.

"Pretty bad," answered Willie, "but not as bad as it will first seem. He took a knock on the head so he ain't conscious jest yet."

"Oh, dear God," whispered Marty, her hand fluttering to her throat, but Willie thought he saw relief showing in her eyes that at least Clark was alive.

"Did ya git the boys?"

"Yes," Willie nodded.

"Thank God," breathed Marty.

Just before the wagon rolled up, Willie placed an arm around each of the women. He wanted just another minute to prepare them.

"Yer pa also has a broken leg," he said to Missie. "We'll need to fix his bed right away. Then fetch some hot water and towels from the kitchen. We want to move him as gentle as we can. Will ya see to it? An', Ma, could ya check to see what we might have around in some disinfectant—he's got some scratches thet we should look after."

With a quick glance toward the now-stopped wagon, the two women ran toward the house to do Willie's bidding.

Willie moved forward.

"Quick," he said to Scottie. "I want him in there an' settled 'fore the women . . ." He did not finish. He did not need to. Scottie understood. Lane rushed out to help them, and with the three men manning the makeshift bed, they got Clark to the house. Missie had already turned down the bed in readiness, but just as Willie had hoped, neither of the women were in the room.

The men laid Clark on the bed and removed his shirt. Wil-

lie found scissors and cut the pant leg from the broken limb.
Scottie had removed the shoes and socks.

"We should bundle him warm against shock," said Lane,
and Willie reached for a flannel nightshirt which they struggled to slip over Clark's head.

"What we gonna do about thet leg?" It was a question they
all had been asking themselves, but it was Lane who finally
voiced it.

"For now we'll jest protect it all we can an' let the women
see him fer a minute," Willie said.

Marty was the first one through the door. She cried out at
the sight of Clark and went to kneel beside him, brushing at
the dirt streaks and bloodstains on his pale face and running
her fingers through his hair. Willie remained silent for a few
minutes and then asked quietly, "Did ya find some disinfectant?"

Marty held up the forgotten bottle.

Missie arrived with a basin of hot water and some towels.
Willie took them from her and she rushed forward to kneel by
her mother. She lifted one of Clark's limp hands and began to
stroke it, willing it to become strong and independent again.

Willie remained silent for a moment and then passed
Marty a small towel.

"Ya want to clean up his face some? Make sure thet the
water isn't too hot. He won't be able to warn ya, and we don't
want a burn."

Marty and Missie both came to life then.

"I'll go fetch a pitcher of cool water," said Missie and fled
from the room. Marty turned to the business of cleaning Clark
up. She looked at his dirty, blood-caked hands, exclaiming
over the bruised knuckles and the palms scratched and dirt-
stained. His nails were broken and dirt-filled from digging
with his fingers.

"My, they be a mess," said Marty, new calmness in her
voice as she set about her task.

Willie sighed with relief and lifted the basin from the chest
so that Missie could add the cold water she had just brought
into the room.

The two women soaked and cleansed the damaged hands and then applied the disinfectant that Marty had produced. They wiped his face and found that, except for a couple of minor scratches, there were no open wounds there. Clark did not stir. Willie observed Marty slyly feeling for a pulse and looking relieved when she actually found one. After Willie was sure that the women had spent enough time with Clark to reassure them, he turned to Missie. "I'm gonna have to ask ya fer a favor now. I know thet it'll be hard to leave yer pa, but I do need to ask ya to care fer a few things fer me."

Missie's eyes widened, but she nodded in agreement.

"Some of the boys were out there diggin' most of the afternoon. They're hungry an' Cookie's already cleared away from the last meal. Could you rustle up a bunch of sandwiches an' some hot coffee fer 'em?"

Missie, surprised, hesitated only a moment. She had never been asked to fix anything for the ranch hands before; Cookie always cared for them no matter what time they came in. But she did not question Willie, only moved to obey.

"Do ya mind givin' her a hand?" Willie asked Marty.

Marty was about to protest and then rose to her feet. Surely this was not too much for Willie to ask.

"The boys have a shift change soon an' gotta git on out to the cattle," Willie went on.

Marty nodded and moved from the room. Willie quickly left the room and went to the boys' room. Josiah was napping and Nathan was playing quietly. Missie had asked him to go to his room before Clark was carried into the house so the small boy would not be unduly frightened concerning his grandfather.

"Hi, fella," greeted Willie as cheerily as the occasion would allow him. "Would ya mind doin' a little chore fer yer pa?"

"Mama said thet I was to stay here 'til she came for me," answered Nathan. And then in deep seriousness he went on, "Did Grandpa git the boys out, Pa?"

"He sure 'nough did," answered Willie, roughing the boy's hair. "But I need ya now. I'll tell yer ma thet I had a job fer ya.

I want ya to run real quick an' tell Cookie an' Scottie thet I need 'em at the house. Tell 'em I need 'em *now*. Then come right back here to yer room. Okay?"

Nathan laid aside his book and ran as his pa bade him. Scottie and Cookie quickly arrived at Clark's room.

"Quick," said Willie. "I've got the ladies busy in the kitchen fixin' a lunch fer the hands."

"Lunch fer the hands?" repeated Cookie in disbelief.

"It was all thet I could think of to git 'em from the room. Now we gotta clean up thet leg, an' we gotta do it quick-like."

The two men nodded and Willie threw back the blankets. The sight that met their gaze was not a pleasant one. For a moment, Willie wished that he could just throw the blanket over the leg again and walk away.

Cookie forgot himself and swore under his breath. " 'Bout the worst one I ever seed," he said. "Even worse shape then my hip was."

"Well, we gotta do what we can. Pass thet there basin." The three men worked over the wound, soaking and cleaning it and then pouring on the whole bottle of disinfectant. Willie tried to straighten the leg so that it didn't lay at such a bizzare angle, but they knew there was nothing they could do to set the bone. After the thorough cleansing, they fixed a loose, makeshift splint and wrapped the damaged leg in it, more to conceal the injury than to do it any good. They were just finishing when Willie heard Missie's quick, light step.

"I take it thet lunch is ready," he whispered to the other two. "Ya go on out an' find someone—anyone—to eat it."

Cookie nodded and went out to round up some cowboys. Scottie, at a nod from his boss, also left the room. He met Missie in the hall.

"I hear tell thet ya fixed some sandwiches, ma'am. Ya mind I wash some of the dirt off me at the cookshack an' I'll be right in. Mighty nice of ya, an' I sure am in need of a cup of coffee. Mighty obliged, ma'am."

Willie covered Clark carefully and picked up the basin with the dirty, bloody water. He held it up high so that Missie couldn't see into it.

"Yer pa seems to be restin' a mite easier now. Thanks fer feedin' the men, Missie. Ya might tell yer ma thet if she wishes to sit with yer pa, the fellas can care fer themselves in the kitchen. An', Missie, I think thet Nathan might need a little reassurance. He must be wonderin' jest what's goin' on. I sent him on a little chore fer me, an' he was 'fraid you'd scold him fer leavin' his room unbidden. Ya might like to peek in and sorta calm him some. I gotta run. Gotta make a little trip. Won't be long."

Missie looked dumbfounded at Willie's announcement, but she nodded mutely and moved toward the boys' room. Willie ached to hold her for a minute, but his hands were occupied with the basin and dirty towels. He sensed that his wife was still in shock.

"Missie," he said softly, "he's gonna be all right. He's tough. As soon as thet little bump on his head . . ." His voice trailed of. Then he went on. "Tell yer ma not to let him move. Iffen he wakes up an' thrashes 'round, call fer Scottie. We couldn't set thet there leg yet, an' he might hurt hisself."

Again Missie nodded silent assent. Willie moved on by her with the basin.

"An', Missie. Try not to worry. I'll be back as soon as I can."

He passed through the door and headed for the bunkhouse and cookshack. He tossed the dirty water to the side of the path. When he reached the cookshack he found Cookie.

"Could only find three riders," said Cookie, "an' even they weren't hungry. Told 'em to eat or else."

"Lane an' Scottie should be hungry," said Willie. "They ain't had anythin' since—"

"This sort of thing takes one's appetite," answered Cookie. "But they'll eat. They'll eat all right, an' they'll drink the coffee. They need the coffee."

Willie passed Cookie the blood-soaked towels. "Think thet ya can clean 'em up some 'fore the ladies see 'em ag'in?"

"Shore," said Cookie and tossed them in a corner.

"Tell Scottie thet I had to go into town. Tell 'im thet I want an eye kept on thet house. Iffen those women need help, I want someone to be there."

Cookie said nothing but his eyes assured Willie that the order would be followed.

Willie strode on down to the corral where he lifted a rope from a post and snaked out his saddle horse. In a few minutes' time the sound of pounding hoofbeats was echoing in the yard.

Marty had had a hard time concentrating on fixing a lunch for the men with Clark lying in the bedroom in his present condition. She couldn't remember how many scoops of coffee to put into the pot nor could she remember where to find bread and butter. Missie's memory didn't seem to be much better, even if it was her own kitchen. Wong was down in the garden selecting vegetables for supper and neither of the ladies thought to call him.

Numbly they went about searching out sandwich materials and spreading the bread. Neither talked, although both were troubled with anxious thoughts that would not be stilled. They worked on in silence until Marty noticed Missie fighting back the tears. She went to her then and took her in her arms.

"He'll be all right. God won't let anythin' happen to 'im. He'll be fine." Oh, how Marty wanted to believe her own words! *They have to be true. They just have to. If anything happens to Clark . . .* Her arms tightened around Missie and she began to pray aloud.

"God, Ya know how we need Ya now. Ya know how we love Clark. Ya know how he has served You. He loves Ya, Lord. An' now we're askin' thet Ya lift him up. Thet Ya give 'im back his mind an' body, iffen it be Yer will, Lord. Amen."

Missie looked at Marty, her eyes wide and the tears streaming down her face. "Oh, Ma!" she cried, "don't pray like that. *Of course* it be His will. Of course it is. He's gotta heal 'im. He's gotta."

Marty too was crying now. "Yer pa always prayed, 'Yer will be done.' "

"You can pray thet iffen ya want to," said Missie insistently, "but I'm gonna tell God exactly what I want. I want Pa. I want him well an' strong ag'in. What's wrong with tellin' God jest what ya want Him to do?"

"Yer pa always says thet we don't be orderin' God; we ask."

Missie pulled away, and Marty could feel frustration and anger in the slim body. Brushing at her tears, Missie went back to the sandwiches. Her whole person seemed shut away. Marty remained silent and began to slice beef and place it on the bread.

When the sandwiches were ready and the coffee had boiled, Missie went to find Willie. Surely her husband would understand and pray with her for Clark's quick recovery. They had not invited Clark west to bring him to harm. But when Missie had met Willie as he was leaving her father's room, he informed her that he was leaving and it seemed that he had no time nor inclination to stop and pray. Willie had suggested that she look in on Nathan to reassure him. Missie went to Nathan's room, but it was Missie who needed some reassurance.

She held the small boy close and let her tears fall. When she was sure that she could speak coherently, she talked to him. "Grandpa got the boys out, Nathan. Grandpa is kind of a hero. He hurt himself saving others. Now he needs to be in bed and have a long rest. You an' Josiah might need to be very quiet an' good for the next few days. Ya can do thet for Grandpa, can't ya?"

She felt Nathan's head bobbing a yes up against her.

"We need to pray for Grandpa. God can make him all better again. Will ya pray with Mama now, Nathan?"

Nathan agreed and the two of them knelt by his bed.

"God," said Nathan simply, "Grandpa got a hero an' is hurt an' needs You to make him better. He needs me an' Josiah to be quiet an' not 'sturb him. Help us to not fight or yell. An' help Mama an' Gram'ma to nurse Grandpa good. Amen."

Missie wished to ask the young boy to pray again. She wanted to say, "Nathan, you didn't ask God to make your grandpa well. You didn't say it, Nathan." Instead she held him for a moment and told him if he'd like to go to the kitchen and share the lunch with the ranch hands, he could. Nathan bounded away, glad to be free of his room.

Missie returned to the kitchen, her heart heavy and her head spinning. How could God answer their prayers if they wouldn't pray them? Missie went to pour the coffee with a shaking hand.

Marty slipped quietly into Clark's room and knelt by his bed. She took one of his hands in hers and caressed it, careful not to bring further hurt to the already damaged hand. It did look better now that it had been cleaned up. She pressed it to her lips and let her tears wash it again.

"Oh, Clark," she whispered, "I couldn't bear it iffen somethin' should happen to you. Oh, God, I jest couldn't stand it. Please, dear God, make 'im better again. Please leave 'im with me. I need 'im so much." There, she was praying the very way she had warned Missie against. Well, she couldn't help it. She couldn't help it! She needed Clark so much. She loved him more than life itself. She couldn't bear to lose him. She just couldn't! "Oh, please, God; please, God," she pleaded.

She stayed beside his bed, crying and praying, until all of her energy and her tears were spent. Clark still did not stir. Would he ever regain consciousness?

At length Marty was aware of a hand on her shoulder. "Mama," asked Missie, "Ya want a cup of coffee?"

Marty shook her head.

"Ya should, ya know. It might be a long night. I told Wong not to bother with supper except for the boys. I didn't think anyone else would be hungry."

Marty looked up. "Yer right," she said wearily. "I couldn't eat a bite."

"Coffee, then," said Missie, holding out the cup.

Marty lifted herself to her feet and took the coffee. She was surprised at how stiff she had become. Unaware that it was getting dark outside, she wondered how long she had been there beside Clark. Missie pushed a chair toward her and she sat down.

"The boys are already in bed," Missie ventured. "Willie still isn't back. Don't know why he—"

"Maybe he went fer a doctor. He said thet yer pa's leg—"

"I'm afraid there's no doctor anywhere around," Missie offered sadly. "He might have heard of someone good at setting breaks though."

Marty sipped at the coffee and watched Missie's face.

"Didn't Willie say where he was goin'?"

"Just said he would be gone for a while an' if we needed anything to call the men. He also said not to let Pa stir around none. Might hurt his leg."

Marty looked at the motionless Clark. "Looks like we needn't worry none 'bout thet. Wish he *would* stir some. It would make me feel some better iffen I could jest talk to him."

"Willie says that movin' might injure his leg even more."

"Maybe it's a blessin' thet he has thet bump on his head. At least he doesn't suffer as much. By the time he comes to again, maybe the pain will be cared fer some."

Marty hadn't thought of the unconsciousness as a blessing, but perhaps it was. She just prayed that it wouldn't last too long.

They sat together in silence. Scottie came for a few minutes and asked if there was anything he could do. They assured him they would call if there was any change.

Cookie hobbled in, his face drained and tired-looking. Missie thought she had never seen him look so old. Maybe he wasn't feeling well; maybe that was why Willie had asked her to make the lunch for the cowboys.

"Cookie, are you all right?" she asked him.

"Whatcha meanin'?" asked Cookie.

"You're lookin' sorta down."

Cookie shook his head. How could he tell her that seeing Clark's injury had reminded him of the injury in his past and the pain that had accompanied it? Clark was truly fortunate right now. He was unaware of pain. But if consciousness returned, would he be able to keep from screaming with the intensity of the agony that he would feel? And how would those earth-rending screams affect the rest of the household? "Guess it bothers me to see a good man hurt," was all that Cookie said.

The evening crawled on. The sun disappeared and the stars came out. Soon a silvery moon was shining down on a familiar world. The horses stomped and fought in the corrals, Max barked at some distant coyotes, the crickets chirped, and the night-winged things beat against the window pane in an effort to get to the light. Still Clark did not stir, and Willie did not come.

Marty and Missie sat together, talking in low tones and praying in turn. At length Missie stood and moved toward the door.

"I think I'll fix somethin' to drink. You be wantin' tea or coffee?"

"Tea, I think," responded Marty wearily. She too stood and walked about the room. Missie left for the kitchen, and Marty moved to pick up Clark's ragged clothes from the floor. She looked at them. They were dirty and torn and the trousers were minus one leg. Clark's leg? She kept forgetting the broken leg in her anxiety over Clark's unconsciousness. But she was not overly concerned about the leg. Many people had suffered broken legs. Usually, with a little skill on the part of some attendant, the leg was soon whole and workable again.

Marty pulled back the bed-cover and looked at the leg swathed in bulky bandages. *Actually, the men did a rather poor job of it,* she thought. She began to unwind the white material, determined to fix the bandage up a bit. To her surprise there was blood on the cloth. Broken legs did not bleed, unless of course the injury was more extensive. Marty unwound the bandage more hurriedly, and the little cry which escaped her lips was like the sound of a small, wounded animal. Clark's leg was not just broken—it was destroyed! Marty felt a sickness sweeping all through her and rushed to the small basin on the stand in the corner. Her whole body shook as she retched. Faint and weak, she grasped the edge of the stand and fought to stand on her feet. At length she regained enough strength and presence of mind to be concerned for the evidence of her sickness before Missie returned. She gathered up the basin and the small pitcher that Missie had used for the cold water and headed for the backyard, disposed of the basin's contents and washed it out and then returned quickly to the room. The cool night air had helped to revive her some and she hastily attempted to put things back in order. Hurriedly she rewrapped the broken limb, trying to copy the men's original bandaging as closely as she could. Then she chided herself. It was not a time for secrets. She knew that Willie had tried to spare her—her and Missie—but the truth needed to be known.

She unwrapped the wound and began to methodically and carefully clean and bind it up, doing the best job possible for her to do. She finished just as Missie returned with the tea.

Marty was glad for the strong, hot tea. She sipped it slowly until she felt some of its strength gradually making its way through her body.

"I took a look at yer pa's leg," she stated matter-of-factly.

"The broken one?"

"The broken one."

"I hope ya didn't move—"

"Yer father did not stir."

A minute of silence followed.

"It's bad, Missie, really bad."

"How bad?"

"A heavy timber or rock must have fallen on it."

"Ya mean. . . ?"

"I mean it's crushed. It'll need a real doctor, one with special skills an' tools—"

"Then we'll find one. Willie prob'ly went for one. That's what he did. He went to find a doctor."

"But ya said—"

"What do I know? Just 'cause I don't know of a doc doesn't mean there isn't one. Willie hears far more—"

"I hope and pray he knows of one."

"He will. He will. Just you wait 'an see. When he gets back here, he'll have—"

The sound of horses came faintly through the window. Missie ran to the door and looked out through the darkness into the yard. No, not horses—a horse. Willie was back, but Willie was alone.

"The doc must be followin'," Missie called to Marty. "Willie is home now."

Missie ran to meet him. When they returned to the house together, Missie's cheeks bore fresh tears. Marty guessed the meaning.

"Willie had them telegraph every town he knew. Nowhere 'round do they have a doctor," she confessed. Willie, standing with slumped shoulders and an ashen face, could not speak.

Marty crossed to him. "You've done all thet ya could," she comforted, putting her hand on his shoulder. "Thanks, Willie." She coaxed forth a smile that she did not feel. "We'll jest have to pray even harder," she said.

Three people now sat in silence, or moved slowly about the room, or spoke in hushed tones. Clark still did not stir through the long night.

When dawn came, Willie insisted that Missie get some rest. The children would be needing her. Missie left to lie down for a brief time. Still no change in Clark. The day moved on, from forenoon to noonday, afternoon to evening. Marty left Clark's side only for a few minutes at a time. She was not interested in eating, could not think of sleeping. Her mind was totally on her husband lying silently in the bed.

Just as the long day ended and the sun was leaving the sky, Clark stirred and a groan came from his lips. Marty rushed to him. He opened his eyes, seemed to recognize her and groaned again. He slipped back into unconsciousness, but to Marty it was a blessed sign. Just to see him move and look at her was something to be thankful for. She allowed the tears to stream down her face as she buried it against him.

Chapter Fifteen

Struggles

Clark remained unconscious the entire next day. Marty stayed by his bed, longing to be able to talk with him. Missie came as often as her duties would allow. In the late afternoon, Willie returned to the house and insisted that both of the ladies take a rest. After a bit of an argument, they went. They realized that they could not carry on longer without some sleep. Willie had Wong bring him coffee, and he settled himself beside Clark's bedside. He had slept very little himself in the last two days. His eyelids felt heavy and his eyes scratchy. He rubbed a calloused hand over his face.

Why did this have to happen? Why? The time they had looked forward to for so long—had dreamed of as a time of joyous reunion—had turned into a nightmare. *Why?* Surely God hadn't brought Clark and Marty way out here to take Clark's life and destroy Marty's faith? It was all a puzzle to Willie.

And the boys? He worried about the boys. They had been so excited about meeting their grandparents. Missie had made

118

it a great adventure for them. They had counted the weeks, the days. And then, when they had met their grandparents, they had loved them so quickly, so deeply—and now this tragedy. Poor little Nathan. Not only had his grandfather been taken from him in the last few days but also his grandmother, and, thought Willie, even his own ma; for Missie's mind was far too unsettled and troubled by her father's condition to be able to do more than care for her children's basic needs.

Willie got up and moved to the boys' room. Josiah slept soundly, unconscious of the burden that this home was presently bearing. Nathan was out. Perhaps he was in the kitchen with Wong or visiting Cookie or playing with Max. The poor little fellow. He was trying so hard to be good.

Willie crossed to his own room and looked in on Missie. Though sleeping, her face was still pale and drawn. Willie's heart ached for her grief.

He gently smoothed back her long hair and left her.

He looked in on Marty. She, too, slept soundly. She looked exhausted—as well she might. She had hardly left Clark's side since the accident had occurred.

Willie went back to Clark's room. He should check the leg. He pulled back the covers and looked at the neat, fresh bandage. This was not the bandage he had hurriedly put on! Someone else had been caring for Clark. Someone else knew of the condition of the leg. Willie wiped his hand over his face again. Did the womenfolk know? He hated the thought of their knowing; and, at the same time, he felt some of the tension leave him. It would be far better if they did know. It would help to prepare them for whatever was ahead.

Willie pulled the light cover up over Clark and sat down heavily in the chair. The house was quiet. Most of its occupants were asleep. Willie, too, dozed occasionally, only to waken chiding himself and determined not to let it happen again.

Josiah woke and left his bed in search of another family member. Willie, hearing him in the hall, went to get him. He picked up the small boy and held him close, walking back and forth in the hallway and crooning words of love to him. Josiah cuddled closely against his father, his pudgy hands around his neck and his fingers intertwined in the heaviness of Willie's hair. He liked to be held. He liked to be loved. As far as Josiah was concerned, the world had no sorrows.

At length, Willie held the little boy away and looked at him. "Are ya hungry?" he asked.

"Yah. Where Mama?"

"Mama is restin'. She's very tired."

"Mama sleepin'?"

"Right. Do you want to go see Wong an' have him git ya some milk an' bread?"

"Yah!" exclaimed Josiah in glee. He always enjoyed a trip to see Wong.

Willie carried him to the kitchen. Wong looked up from the table where he and Nathan were cutting doughnuts.

"Aha," said Wong, "small boy is wake now."

"Awake an' hungry, Wong. Ya think ya might have somethin' fer him?"

Wong smiled. He enjoyed the children.

"Yes, yes. Wong find."

Nathan called to Josiah. "Hi, Joey. Ya all done with yer sleep? See what big brother is doin'. Look! I'm helpin' Wong make doughnuts. We're gonna have 'em fer supper."

"Maybe. Maybe not," said Wong. "Too slow. Maybe tomorrow."

"I'll hurry," said Nathan and began to slap down the cutter in rapid succession, making queer-shaped doughnuts with chopped-out sides as one cut overlaid another.

"Slow. Slow," called Wong. "We have some for supper. You make slow."

Nathan slowed down. Willie squeezed the boy's shoulder. "I can hardly wait," he said. "Those shore look like good doughnuts." Then he turned to Wong.

"Speakin' of supper, ya wanna jest feed the boys? The women are both havin' a sleep, an' I plan to let 'em sleep as long as they can. The boys can play outside fer a while an' then they can eat. I'll jest have a bowl of soup or some stew in the bedroom."

Wong nodded.

Willie returned to the bedroom and took his place beside Clark. There was no change.

The hours crawled by slowly. Cookie came in and stayed with Clark while Willie washed his sons and readied them for bed. He spent extra time with them, holding them and reading to them, and then he tucked them in and remained in their room until they had both dropped off to sleep.

When he returned to the sickroom, he was surprised to hear Clark groaning. Cookie was bending over him, trying to restrain him from movement.

"He's comin' out of it," said Cookie. "Don't be surprised iffen there is some screamin'."

Clark moaned again and fought against his extreme pain. He was not aware enough to realize yet where the pain was coming from.

"Don't know how he's gonna stand it when he wakes up a bit more," Cookie muttered, and Willie had the impression that Cookie knew firsthand what he was talking about.

Willie feared what Clark's cries might do to his sleeping household.

"Isn't there anythin'—?"

"Ya watch 'im," said Cookie. "I'm gonna find Scottie."

Cookie hobbled out, and Scottie soon came noiselessly into the room, breathless from running. Willie watched as he pulled out a small package from his pocket to open it. Willie did not see the contents of the package, nor did he ask any questions; but Scottie seemed to feel that some information was in order.

"A little morphine. Cookie's. He needs it now an' then fer the pain thet still bothers 'im. Makes me keep it so thet he won't be tempted to take it oftener than he should."

Willie nodded.

Clark was thrashing and moaning, his brow covered with perspiration; his hands clutched at the bedclothes as if to tear away the pain. Scottie leaned over him and spooned the drug into his mouth. It was awhile before it took effect, and the men guarded and soothed Clark as they waited for the medicine to work. At last Clark became quieter and eventually fell into a deep sleep. Willie was thankful for the respite; but what would they do when Cookie's small supply of morphine ran out?

It was almost morning before Clark woke again. Willie had been dozing in the chair and was awakened by Clark's moaning. Clark's eyes were open when Willie looked up at him; and, though the pain would have been considerable, Clark was rational.

He looked at Willie and, for the first time in three days, seemed to be aware of his situation.

Willie was relieved to realize that Clark was alert. At least his mind had not been affected.

"How ya doin'?" asked Willie softly and lifted some water to Clark's lips.

Clark sipped very little and then turned his head. A groan escaped him.

"Pain," was all he said. "Pain."

"Where does it hurt the most?" persisted Willie. He had to know the extent of the head injury.

"Leg," said Clark.

Willie felt a measure of relief pass through him.

"How's yer head?"

"Hazy . . . little ache . . . all right."

"Good."

Clark rolled his head back and forth, the moans escaping from his throat.

"Where's Marty?" he finally asked.

"I made her go sleep fer a while."

This satisfied Clark. He lay clenching his jaw to keep the screams from coming. Willie knew that he needed more medication and moved the lamp to the window, their prearranged signal.

"How long?" Clark gasped out.

"You've been here fer three nights. It happened the afternoon of the day before."

"The old mine . . . I remember."

It was a good sign. Willie breathed a thankful prayer.

"How are the boys?"

"Haven't heard much since we brought you out," said Willie and let it go at that.

"Did ya get Abe out?"

"His pa did."

"Good."

Clark tried to fight away the pain so that he could sleep again, but it didn't work. Scottie was soon there, and Clark took the medication without protest. This time he did not sleep as soundly. He dozed off and on. The pain was still with him, but he was able to bear it.

"Didn't give 'im as much," Scottie whispered to Willie. "We gotta ration this here stuff out."

Willie nodded.

The light from the dawn was gently coloring the morning sky. Clark slept, then spoke and slept again. Willie knew that Marty was anxious for a word with her husband. Perhaps she had slept enough and needed to be called.

"Scottie, can ya stay a few minutes with 'im? I should wake Mrs. Davis. She'll want to see 'im." Scottie nodded.

Willie woke Marty gently.

"He's awake now. Not too much awake, but he's able to talk some."

Marty threw back the quilt that covered her fully clothed body and bounded from the bed.

Willie attempted to slow her down. He took her arm.

"He's in awful pain, Ma. It ain't easy to see 'im like thet."

Marty nodded dumbly, but her step did not slow.

When they reached Clark's room, Scottie stepped outside; and Marty threw herself at Clark's bedside and began to weep against him.

He reached out a trembling hand and soothed her hair. He let her cry. He knew her well enough to know that she needed that. When her tears were spent, he spoke to her.

"I'm all right. Don't fret yerself."

"Shore," she smiled, blinking away tears. "Shore ya are."

"My leg's not too good, though. Ya knowin' thet?"

"I know." The way Marty said it made Willie aware that

she truly did know. Marty must have been the one who had changed the bandages. Once again, Willie felt a surge of respect for the strength of this woman.

Clark ran a feeble hand through Marty's tangled hair.

"Yer not lookin' yer best, Mrs. Davis," Clark teased her.

"Thet's funny," said Marty, smiling through tears, "ya ain't never looked better."

Willie left them.

Chapter Sixteen

More Struggles

Scottie was there to portion out small amounts of the morphine as Clark needed it. Clark really could have used far more painkiller than he was allowed, but once their supply was gone there would be no more.

Clark was able to talk with his visitors. Nathan even was allowed a short visit with his grandpa. He was awed to see his strong grandfather lying pale and still on the bed; but when Clark teased him and rumpled his hair, Nathan felt reassured. Marty and Missie both spent their time trying to think of something they could do to ease Clark's pain or restore his body. Missie fussed in the kitchen over special dishes that she hoped would tempt her father's appetite. He tried to eat to please her, but it was difficult for him to swallow the food with the dreadful pain always present throughout his whole body.

Word came from town concerning the boys who had been involved in the disaster. Andy seemed to be recovering. His broken ankle had not been crushed, and his parents felt that it would heal with time. They were deeply grateful to Clark for his courageous rescue.

Funeral services were held for Abe. Marty hardly knew how to tell Clark, but she felt that he deserved to know. She approached the subject cautiously.

"They say thet Andy's leg should be healin'."

"Thet's good," said Clark. "The way thet timber had 'im pinned, I was a-feared thet it might be bad broke."

"The other boy—Casey—he's fine. Jest some scrapes an' scratches an' his deep inner hurts, I guess. The third boy, Abe, was his younger brother."

"He told me."

"Abe didn't make it, Clark."

"I know." Clark spoke very quietly.

"Ya know?"

"He was already dead when I first found him."

Marty was surprised and, for a moment, angry. "Ya *knew* he was dead when ya risked everythin' to go back on in there an'—"

Clark hushed her. "If it had been our boy, would ya have wanted him out?"

Marty was silent. Yes, if it had been her boy, she would have wanted to hold him one more time.

Marty was relieved at the clearness of Clark's mind. She was so glad that the head injury had not caused permanent damage, but she could not shut from her mind the picture of Clark's leg and the condition it was in. Each time she entered the sickroom, the stench of the injured leg met her with increasing force. The leg was in bad shape; it might even claim Clark's life. Marty fought that thought with all of her being. They needed medicine. They needed a doctor. At times, she was tempted to demand that Willie hurry them to the train so they might head for home. In more rational moments, Marty knew the length of the trip and the weakened condition of Clark would certainly snuff out his life.

And then Clark began to flush with fever. His eyes took on a glassy look, and his skin was hot and dry. *It's the poison*, admitted Marty. *It's the poison from the wound.*

Marty could hardly bear this new dilemma. He had been

doing well. He had been gaining back a little strength. He had even been able to talk. And now this. They had no way to fight this. *Oh, dear God, what can we do?*

At first, they did not talk about Clark's condition; for to talk about it would be to admit it, and also to admit that they were defeated, for they had nothing with which to fight the dreaded killer.

At last Marty knew they could no longer try to pretend that the problem was not there.

"Bring me a pan of hot water," she said to Missie. "An' boil a good, sharp pair of yer best scissors. We've gotta do somethin' 'bout yer father's leg."

Then Marty went to find Scottie. Willie and Scottie had thought the drug ministrations to Clark had been unnoticed by Marty, so Scottie was caught off guard when Marty walked up to where he was working on the cinch of a saddle and calmly announced, "Scottie, I don't know how much medicine thet ya still have left, but Clark needs a good-sized dose now. I've got to clean up thet leg the best thet I can or it's gonna kill 'im. The poison from thet gangrene is goin' all through his system an' we don't have much time."

Scottie looked at the small figure before him. She was nobody's fool. She also had more inner strength than any woman he knew. In no way would he be able to stomach the cleaning up of the offensive leg.

He went for the medicine and gave Clark a large dose. Marty waited until the medicine had taken effect, then gathered together all of her limited supplies and every ounce of her courage and went to Clark's room. She threw the window wide open and lit a small piece of rag to help with the odor and then threw back the light quilt and removed the bandages. It was even worse than she had feared. Never before had Marty faced such a sight and smell. She wanted to faint, to go be sick; but she would allow herself neither. She soaked and snipped and cut away dead flesh, but even as she worked she knew that she was fighting a losing battle. She finished her difficult task, knowing that what she had done would not be enough.

Gently she covered Clark, all but the damaged leg. She left

it exposed to the air, thinking that the air might somehow do it some good. Then she cleaned the scissors and knife that she had used and put things away in their proper places and went to her own bed.

Down upon her knees, she cried out her anguish to God. She began by telling Him how much Clark meant to her and reminding God of how faithfully Clark had served Him over the years. She told God that she had already suffered through the loss of one husband and couldn't possibly bear to lose another. She reminded the Lord of her family at home and of Missie and the grandchildren here. They too needed Clark. And then she pleaded and finally demanded that God heal her husband. Hadn't He promised to answer the prayers of His children when they prayed in faith, prayed believing?

Then she returned to Clark. Clark's breathing was just as shallow, his face just as flushed, his brow just as hot as before; but Marty determined that she would sit right beside him and wait for the Lord's miracle.

Missie came in. At the sight of her father's infected leg, she gave a little cry and, placing her hand over her mouth, ran from the room. Marty's heart ached for her. *What would she ever have done if she'd seen it 'fore I cleaned it up?* thought Marty. Marty was thankful Missie had been spared at least that much.

Missie too went to her room and fell down beside her bed. "Oh, God," she prayed. "Ya can't let Pa die. Ya can't! Please, God. Please." Missie was unable to do more than tearfully plead.

In Clark's room, the drug began to wear off. Clark tossed and turned in his pain. Marty bathed his hot face and body in an attempt to get the fever down. It had little effect. Clark soon became delirious, and Marty had to call for help to hold him. Willie came and then Cookie, and the two men sent Marty from the room. Marty paced back and forth, back and forth, praying that God's miracle might soon come. Still Clark's screams and groans reached her ears.

Maria came. White-faced and wide-eyed, she stood in the hallway and talked to the tearful Missie. She did not stay long. The agony of Clark and the distress of the total household drove her crying from the home.

The hours crawled by. Marty went to the sickroom occasionally, but Clark's misery was more than she could bear. At last, she went to her room again, and again fell beside her bed. This time her prayer was different.

"Oh, God!" she cried. "Ya know best. I can't stand to see 'im suffer so. I love 'im, God. I love 'im so. Iffen Ya want to take 'im, then it's all right. I won't be blamin' Ya, God. Ya know what's best. I don't want 'im to suffer, God. I leave 'im in Yer hands. Yer will be done, whether it's healin' or takin', thet's up to You, God. An', God, whatever Yer will, I know thet Ya'll give me—an' all of us—the strength thet we need to bear it."

Marty arose from her knees and went to find Missie. A strange peace filled Marty. She still shivered with each scream from Clark. It still pierced her very soul to know that he suffered so, but Marty knew that God was in control and that His divine will would be done.

She found Missie in the boys' room. The boys were not there. They had been taken to the barn by Lane so that they might not hear the agonizing cries of their grandfather.

Missie clutched the small harness that Clark had used to carry her as an infant and that she in turn had used to carry her own sons. She was sobbing out her hurt and anguish.

"Missie," Marty said, taking the girl into her arms. "It's gonna be all right. I know it is."

Missie burst into fresh tears. "Oh, I wanna believe that. I've been prayin' an' prayin' for God to make him well."

"He may not," said Marty simply.

Missie looked at her mother in bewilderment.

"But ya said—"

"I said it will be all right. An' it will. Whatever God decides to do will be the best. He knows us. He knows our needs. He seeks our good. Whatever He wills—"

But Missie pushed away her arms.

"Oh, Missie, Missie," sobbed Marty. "I fought it too. I fought it with all my bein'. I want yer pa. I want him here with

130

me. But God knows thet. I don't even have to tell 'im. But, little girl, we've got to trust Him. We've gotta let God truly be God.''

Missie rose and left the room, still sobbing. Marty heard her close the door on her own room and throw herself on the bed. There was nothing more that Marty could say. She could only pray.

Marty went to the kitchen to ask Wong for coffee for the men in the sickroom. Clark had been given another opportunity of rest. The last of the medication had been given. Each one in the house felt the lingering question of "what then—?"

As Marty carried the pot of coffee and cups to the room, she met Missie in the hall. Her face was still tear-streaked but more serene. "Mama," she said, "I just wanted you to know that it's all right. I've prayed it all through, an' I'm . . . I'm willin' to . . . to let God be God. He does know best. I knew it all along. It's just easy to forget sometimes when you want your own way so—" She could go no further.

Marty managed a weak smile, and the tears flowed down her cheeks. She leaned over and kissed Missie on the cheek and then moved to go on to the room where Clark lay.

Missie wiped her tears on her apron and straightened up just as a knock sounded on the door.

Missie went to answer. Maria stood there, her shoulders square and her eyes shining with faith and pride. And just behind her stood Juan.

"Can we come in?" she asked. "My husband . . . is a doctor.''

Chapter Seventeen

Juan

Juan walked purposefully into the sickroom and set his case on the bed. His quick glance took in Clark's pallor and the flush that colored his cheeks. His nose caught the stench of rotting flesh, and he turned to the leg.

He knew even before he looked just what he would find. The crushed limb was badly infected, and the gangrene was not only eating away the flesh of the leg but was also poisoning the body of the man. The leg would have to be removed.

Juan's thoughts went back to another time, one just like this one. Another man lay before him with a similar leg and, at that time as well, Juan the doctor had needed to make a life-saving decision. He had decided then, as he was deciding now, that the leg must be sacrificed in order to save the life. All of his training and experience told him so. He had done what he needed to do. The man had lived.

And then . . . Juan shuddered as other memories crowded into his mind. The angry screams, the raging accusations, the shouts that spoke of betrayal, and finally the sound of a pistol

131

shot. For a moment, Juan felt that he must flee Clark's room—and the memories. Then the groans of the sick man and the cries of the women in the hall strengthened him. He straightened himself and looked at the two men in the room.

"I'm going to need lots of boiling water and a strong man to assist me," he said evenly and removed his jacket.

"I wish thet I could volunteer," said Willie. "I'd like to, but I'm a-feared thet I'd cave in halfway through. I can see to the water, an' I'll find ya a man."

Willie told the ladies about the need for boiling water and went on to the bunkhouse. Lane was sitting in the doorway watching Nathan and Josiah who played with Max.

Willie went to the bunkhouse, motioned Lane inside, and shut the door.

"We found us a doc," he said; and, at the surprise that showed on everyone's faces, he continued. "Juan. Juan has all the trainin' an' has even been in practice fer a few years. I know ya all have questions. So do I, but now ain't the time fer answers. We'll git 'em all in good time. Right now I need a man. I got a job thet won't be easy to do. The doc needs help. He's gonna take off thet there leg. Yer wonderin' why I don't offer, him bein' my father-in-law an' all. Well, I'll tell ya straight out. I'm not sure thet I could take it. I might fold up on the doc jest when he needed me most. Anyone here thet thinks he could do it?"

Willie's eyes looked around the bunkhouse. Not all of the cowboys were in. Some of them were out on the range taking their shift with the cattle. Those who were in the room probably wished they were far away as well, mending fence or herding doggies. Willie had asked a hard thing.

Jake lay stretched out on his bunk, catching up on some sleep. He had had the late shift the night before. In the corner, Smith, the bitter, critical member of the crew, sat smoking a cigarette and staring at the cards in his hand. Browny was his partner in the game. Clyde, who sat on a stool near the window, shifted the lariat he was working on into the other hand and shot tobacco juice at the bean can sitting on the floor. Lane went white and stared at his hands as though trying to measure whether they would be capable of such a job. The room was heavy with silence. At last, Lane cleared his throat and spoke softly. "I'll go."

"Ya sure?"

Lane nodded his agreement.

"It won't be easy."

Lane recognized that.

"Wish I could help ya—I can't promise. Yer sure ya can do it?"

Lane swallowed. "I know *I* can't," he said solemnly. "But I'm . . . I'm trustin' thet *He* can."

The religion-hating Smith looked at the silent, shy Lane with grudging respect.

Willie and Lane went to the house where the doctor was waiting. Willie led the group in prayer, and the men went to Clark's room and the ladies to the kitchen.

The hands on the clock seemed to drag their way around. The three women sat at a small worktable, untouched coffee cups before them. They had prayed together off and on throughout the whole ordeal. They had cried together and praised together. Maria felt that it was time to share her secret.

"Juan always wanted to be a doctor. From the time he was a small boy, he dreamed and planned. At first his father said no. If he wanted to serve, he could be a priest and serve the church; but Juan pleaded. Finally his father said, 'Yes, go ahead; but you will need to pay your own way. My money will not go for foolish dreams.' His father is very wealthy. In his own way, he loves his sons. He wanted both of his boys to stay and ranch with him. Juan went away to the city to school. It was hard. He had to work and he had to study. His father thought that he would give up and come home again. But Juan did not. At last he was finished. He was a doctor and was given a good job in a city hospital. His father thought that he should come home now. He could be a doctor to the gringos and their families, but Juan said no, he must first know more, and then he would come home."

Maria stopped. It was very difficult for her to continue.

"And then one day he was called home. It was urgent. He must go home right away. A man had been hurt. Juan went home and found the injured man. He, too, had crushed his leg. A horse had fallen on him. The leg was too badly broken to fix. It might have been different if he had quickly had a doctor and had been taken to a hospital soon. By the time Juan got there, the leg was as this one. It was infected and was stealing away the man's life."

Maria stopped again and took a deep breath.

"He had to take the man's leg. He had to. There was no other choice. Juan did the only thing that he could do. The man lived and he became again awake. And then . . . then a dreadful thing happened. He discovered that his leg was gone. He was angry. He screamed at Juan. He wanted to kill him. He said that Juan had always been jealous of him and had used his knife to make him less a man. He screamed and screamed until the father came. He too was angry. He sent Juan from the room. And then . . . then there was a pistol shot. Juan ran back to the room. The man had shot himself. Juan's father had not stopped him. The father lay weeping across the body of the dead man—his son—Juan's brother."

Missie gasped in horror and Marty shut her eyes against the awfulness of the story that Maria had told.

"Juan left his father's home and said that he would never, never be a doctor again. He hated what he had done to his family. He came to me. I loved him very much. We were planning to be married. Juan said that he could not marry me, that he was going far away. That he would never again be a doctor. He threw his bag across the yard and wept as he told me. I said that I loved him. That I still wanted to marry him. That I would go away with him. At last he said I could go. I packed a few things and we went to the village priest who married us. Juan did not know it, but I packed his medicine bag as well. It has been hidden these many years.

"We came here and we began to ranch. Juan knew ranching. He had been raised on one of the biggest ranches of Mexico. He had ridden and cared for cattle from the time he was a small niño. But still Juan was not happy. He could not forget the past. He could not hide the desire to be a doctor."

Maria toyed with the handle of the cup that held the cold coffee.

"I said that Juan was troubled about coming to church. Of what to teach our little ones. That is right. I did not lie. But Juan is also troubled about other things. He looks at the boy with the twisted arm, and it turns a knife within him. He knows that he could have set the arm properly and the boy would not have been crippled. He knows of the boy with the broken ankle in town. He knows that you all suffer here in this house with the good man, Clark. It makes my Juan suffer, too. He has not slept or eaten the last several days. He did not know what to do. He did not know that I had his bag and there was some medicine in it."

Maria sighed.

"He will always ask himself, could he have saved the leg if he had come sooner?"

"No," said Marty. "He mustn't think that. The leg was crushed. It was a very bad break. I don't think thet anyone could have saved it. I pretended—but I didn't really believe. Juan mustn't blame hisself. He mustn't. He mustn't blame hisself 'bout his brother either. Juan did what had to be done. He couldn't have done anythin' else."

Maria smiled weakly. "I know that and you know that—and down deep Juan knows that, too. But it still torments him. Only now—now I pray that he can forget that deep hurt and go on to heal. He was always meant to be a healer, my Juan."

Willie walked into the kitchen. His face was pale and his hands shaky.

"It's all over," he said. "Doc says it went well. Now we jest haf to wait an' see."

Marty rose to hurry to Clark, and Missie and Maria prayed together again.

Chapter Eighteen

Healing

During the next few days, Clark was in and out of consciousness, mostly because of the medication that he was given. Dr. De la Rosa, as he was now known, stayed with him, Maria having returned home to their children. Marty found the time following Clark's surgery even more taxing than her previous vigil, but Juan gave her encouraging reports daily. Clark's pulse was more normal and his color was improving. Juan was hopeful that the infection had been caught in time. Marty dreaded the time when Clark would be aware of the fact that his leg was missing. She worried about how he might respond to the shocking truth.

It happened on the third day following surgery. Clark awoke and seemed to be quite rational. He asked for Marty, who was at the time having her lunch. She went to him, and Dr. De la Rosa left the room.

"I'll be right here in the hall if you need me," Juan whispered softly as he left.

Marty crossed to Clark's bed.

"Hello, there," she said. "It's nice to see ya awake. You've been sleepin' a powerful lot lately."

Clark managed a crooked grin. "I reckon," he admitted.

"Ya feelin' some better?"

"I think thet I'm feelin' lots better than even I know," said Clark.

"Meanin'?"

"Meanin' I've sorta lost track of time an' what's been goin' on. I need a few explanations, Marty. Seems I've been in an' out of a nightmare. Care to fill me in?"

Marty sighed heavily. "It's been a nightmare fer all of us—but I guess fer you, most of all."

Marty did not go on. Clark waited for her a moment and then prompted. "I think thet I need to know, Marty."

"Where do ya want to start?"

"How 'bout the beginnin'?"

"Ya remember the mine accident?"

"I remember."

"Ya know thet ya was hit on the head an' were out fer a few days?"

"I do."

"Do ya remember comin' 'round at all?"

"Yah. It's sorta hazy. I was in an awful lot of pain. My leg was—"

Clark stopped for a moment, then went on. "My leg's not as bad now."

"We found a doctor. He's been carin' fer ya."

"A doctor! Since I woke up, Juan's been—"

"Juan is a doctor."

"Juan?"

"Right."

"Well, don't thet beat all?" grinned Clark. "How'd thet all come 'bout?"

"It's a long story," said Marty. "Juan's been runnin' away from his past. One day I'll tell it all to ya."

"Well, iffen thet don't beat all," Clark said again. "Juan a doctor. Folks here 'bout must be crazy-happy to learn—"

"They's excited 'bout it, all right. Soon's yer well enough

to leave behind, Juan is headin' fer a city to git what he needs to start up a proper-like practice. He's already set the ankle of thet boy in town who was in the mine. He thinks thet he might even be able to re-break an' set the arm of the young Newton child. The parents are willin' fer 'im to try."

"Well, I'll be," said Clark and then, after a moment of silent thoughtfulness, he went on. "Ya know, this here accident might be worth it iffen it got a doctor fer this town. Iffen it helped clear up Juan's problems so thet he could do his proper work ag'in, it jest might be worth the price."

Marty cringed. Clark did not as yet know just how high the price had been.

"So Juan cared for me, huh?" went on Clark.

"He did," answered Marty, "right when we had 'bout given up."

"I was thet bad?"

"Thet bad."

"He had the proper medicine?"

"Enough fer it to do the job. Heard him fussin' thet he didn't have somethin' else, but I guess what he *did* have worked."

"An' he fixed my leg."

"He saved yer life," said Marty.

"He fixed my leg an' saved my life."

Marty did not answer. She bit her lip and then she realized that Clark was waiting for her to go on.

"Clark," she said slowly, "yer leg was bad broke. It wasn't just a break, Clark; it was crushed. Then it got even worse. It got all gangrene. The gangrene nearly killed ya. It would have, too, iffen it hadn't been fer Dr. De la Rosa."

Clark's face had gone white as Marty talked. The words *gangrene* and *poison* seemed to linger in his eyes and on his lips.

"An' yer sayin'—?"

"I'm sayin' thet Dr. De la Rosa fixed yer leg as best he could—in the only way he could. He took it off, Clark. He took it off 'fore it killed ya."

Clark turned away his face. Marty saw a deep shiver vibrate all through him. She threw her arms around him and held him close. She waited for a moment until the truth had time to slowly penetrate his thinking.

"Clark," she said, her tears falling freely, "I know thet isn't what ya wanted to hear. I know thet ya didn't want to lose a leg. I didn't want it either, Clark. With my whole bein', I fought it. But it was yer leg or *you*. For a while, it looked like it would be both. Oh, Clark, I'm jest so thankful to God thet He sent a doctor along in time to spare ya. I . . . I . . . I don't know how I'd ever made it without you, Clark. God spared ya, an' I'm so glad. So glad. We'll git by without the leg . . . I promise."

Clark smoothed her hair and held her close. His trembling eventually stopped. He could even speak.

"Yer right. It'll be all right. Guess it jest takes some gettin' used to." And then Marty just let herself go and cried out all of her pent-up worries and frustrations. "Oh, Clark," she sobbed. "I'm sorry. So sorry thet it had to happen to you like this. Iffen I could have jest taken yer place . . . I know how important it be to a man to be whole—to be able to feed an' care fer his family. I could have done my carin' from a chair. It wouldn't have mattered near as much to me. Oh, Clark! I'm so sorry."

"Hush now, hush," said Clark. "Yer actin' like a hysterical woman. This don't change things. I can still be a-carin' fer my family. One leg ain't gonna make a lot of difference. Hush now. Iffen the Lord hadn't a figured thet I could do without thet there leg, He wouldn't have 'llowed this, now would He?"

At length, Clark got Marty comforted and in control. He pushed her gently away from him. "An' now," he said, "iffen ya don't mind, I'm feelin' in the need fer some rest. I'll talk to ya in the mornin'. Now ya send thet there doc back in here, will ya?"

Marty left the room and sent in Juan. Juan entered the room, his pulse racing. He remembered the other incident when his brother had discovered his missing limb. He didn't blame any man for taking the news hard. He stood silently, looking at the big man lying still on the bed. Clark was the first to speak.

"I heard thet I owe ya my life." Juan said nothing. Perhaps

Clark did not yet know about his leg.

But Clark went on. "It must be a powerful hard decision fer a man to make—even a man trained in medicine—to take a man's limb an' spare the man's life, or let him die with both legs on. I'm glad thet I've never had to do the choosin'. I want to tell ya 'thank you' for bein' brave enough to make the choice fer me when I wasn't able to make it fer myself. I would have chosen to live, Juan—even without the leg—I would have chosen to live. Life is good—an' life is in the hands of Almighty God. Now, I'm not sayin' thet I fancy learnin' to live without a leg. I'm not pretendin' to be some hero thet it won't bother none. But I am sayin' 'thank you' fer givin' me thet chance. With God's help, I'll make it. If He 'llowed it, then He must have a plan to git me through it, too. Fer He plans only fer my good."

Juan stood watching Clark, not speaking. There were no angry cries, no cursing, no incriminations coming from Clark. He knew of his handicap—he knew of his loss—but he had accepted it and even thanked the doctor for giving him a chance to live. There was a difference here. A distinct difference between the way this man acepted his handicap and the way his own brother had. What made the difference? Juan determined to do some thinking on it when he could get off by himself and take the time. One thing he already knew—where his brother had cursed God, this man thanked God. Perhaps . . . perhaps it had something to do with that.

Clark interrupted his thoughts.

"An' now, doctor, I don't be pretendin' thet this here hasn't shook me up a bit. It's gonna take some thinkin' on to git used to the idea. I don't much feel up to thinkin' at the moment. Ya happen to have somethin' to help a man git a little sleep instead? I think thet it might be easier to handle come mornin'."

Dr. De la Rosa moved to prepare some medication.

Clark did not go to sleep immediately. He spent time thinking, even though he wished that he could shove the whole problem off to the side and pretend that it did not exist. He also did some praying—deep, soul-searching praying—asking for God's help in the hours of adjustment and growing. He even did some weeping—heart-rending weeping—with sobs that shook his large frame. When it was all over, he wiped away the tears from his gaunt cheeks, set his chin, and reached for the unseen hand of God. He never discussed his inner feelings concerning his handicap again.

Chapter Nineteen

Adjustments

Marty often thought that Clark's recovery was slow indeed, but to Dr. De la Rosa, it was a daily miracle. Clark was
doing much better than the doctor had dared even to hope.
When one considered what the man had been through, his
convalescence was truly amazing.

Willie had kept the family in the East informed throughout the whole ordeal by the means of telegrams. A great measure of relief accompanied the cable assuring them that Clark
was well on the way to recovery. He stated that, at the present, he was still unable to give them a date for Clark's return
home. The answer soon came, "Pa, don't hurry. Everything
fine here. Letter following." Marty anxiously waited for the
arrival of the letter.

As she sat mending one of Nathan's small shirts, Marty
was surprised to discover that it was well past the time they
had planned to have returned to their farm. How different the
trip had turned out from what they had expected it to be!
Marty quickly realized that Clare's wedding was only days

away. She and Clark would not—could not—possibly make it back in time for the wedding. Deep disappointment flooded through Marty. She would hate to miss the wedding, but neither would she want the young couple to postpone it on their account. Then Marty thought of Luke's plans to go off to college. She should be home right now preparing his clothes and getting him ready. How she hated to miss that! A few unbidden tears slipped down and Marty wiped them away quickly before they could be observed. But Luke was so young. It was hard enough to let him go, but without her there to— She stopped herself. She'd be crying in earnest if she didn't get herself under control.

Marty laid aside the shirt and went to check on Clark. Missie was already there. In fact, it was not often that Missie was *not* with her father. She made up games that she played with him, she read to him, she fluffed his pillows and sponged his face and hands, she talked to him about her garden and her children, she discussed his meals and she told of happenings in the district. Yes, Missie was often with her father. It was touching to see so much love between father and daughter. Marty smiled at the two of them.

"Ya know what he's a-sayin'?" said Missie in exasperation. "He's sayin' that he's gonna get up."

Marty smiled again. "I think thet's a great idea," she said.

"Great?" Missie, in shock, exclaimed. "He's not ready for that yet! Juan said—"

"Juan said thet he should choose his own pace. Iffen yer father thinks thet he is—"

Clark stopped the two of them. "Hold it, hold it," he said, raising his hands in his customary way. "No use ya all gittin' into it. I will obey my doctor. I will not git up 'til I am ready to git up. Iffen ya don't think thet the time is right, Missie, I will wait."

Missie looked relieved, and Marty looked slightly bewildered.

"I will wait until right after lunch," continued Clark.

Missie sputtered, "Big wait—especially since it's now eleven-thirty."

Then they all three began to laugh.

After lunch, Clark sat on the edge of the bed for a while. Later, with Marty on one side and Wong on the other, he moved to the porch to sit in a rocking chair. The day was warm, and the sun's rays felt good to the man who had been shut away in the house far too long. He took great breaths of the fresh air and sniffed deeply of the earth and the growing things.

Nathan came to play by him, showing him all the tricks Max could do. Being more a family dog than a showdog, Max had very few of them, so Nathan put him through the same ones over and over while Clark laughed appreciatively as though enjoying each trick.

Scottie just then returned from town and with him was the letter from the family back home.

"Dear Ma and Pa," Marty read aloud.

"We are so glad to hear that Pa is finally feeling better. We can't say how sorry we are for the accident that took Pa's leg, but we are so glad that he was spared. We have all been praying daily, I guess almost hourly, for you both.

"We don't want you to worry none about things here at home. Clare has decided to go ahead with his wedding. They had talked of waiting until you were back home again, but they thought that that might pressure you into traveling before you are really ready. We want to be good and sure that you are strong enough for the trip before you attempt it, Pa. So, for our sake, please don't come home until you are really well.

"Arnie is taking good care of the stock. That's been his job since you left, Pa. Of course he helps Clare in the field, too, but the stock is in his special care. He has not been seeing Hester lately. Her brothers just made it too miserable, and she says that she doesn't want to marry anyone that her brothers can't drink with.

"There's a new girl in town though. She is the new preacher's daughter, and Arnie has gotten pretty friendly with her. You would really like her, Ma. She's a very thoughtful person, and Arnie is beginning to think that she's kind of cute.

"Luke's not going to college this fall. He's been seeing Dr. Watkins a lot lately. Dr. Watkins says that he's still lots young and another year of waiting won't hurt him any. Dr. Watkins is giving Luke the use of some of his medical books to read. He is taking Luke with him on his Saturday calls too, so Luke says he is learning more than he ever would in the first year of school. Dr. Watkins really seems to be enjoying Luke. He treats him as though he was his son. Guess Dr. Watkins maybe misses not having a family of his own. Anyway, Luke seems really happy with this arrangement.

"Everything is going well here. The canning is most all done, Ma. The garden has done real good and the apples are coming on well. Ma Graham came over and helped me for one day. She sends her love. Everyone at church is remembering you in prayer.

"Nandry and Clare both say that they will write now that we know a little better what to say. I will admit that we were really scared for awhile. God bless you both. We miss you to be sure, but we are doing fine on our own.

"In love, Ellie and the boys"

The letter both relieved and saddened Marty. She missed them all so much, but it was good to hear that they were all right and managing well without them. She was glad that Clare was going ahead with the wedding, and she was also glad that Arnie had a nice girl for a friend. Marty was relieved to hear that her Luke would not be going off to college without his mother there to see him off. She thanked God for working out these things and for allowing Dr. Watkins to shepherd the boy.

Clark turned from the letter with relief in his face. Marty had been unaware that, in spite of his ordeal, he also was concerned for the family at home.

"Well," he said, "seems as though they be makin' do jest fine without us. I'm proud of the young'uns you've raised, Mrs. Davis."

Marty beamed. "An' so am I. 'Course you didn't have much of a hand in it at all."

"Maybe we can jest sort of take our time recuperatin' after all," sighed Clark. His grin was a little wobbly. "I think I'll jest go on back to my bed and catch me a nap."

Marty looked at him quickly and saw that he was rather pale. Maybe Missie *had* been right; maybe Clark was pushing things too quickly.

But Clark was content to take one day at a time. He attempted only what he thought he could manage. Very gradually, his strength was returning.

Chapter Twenty

Neighbors

The two families from town whose boys had been involved in the old mine accident came out to the LaHaye farm for a visit. The ladies, still unable to talk of the incident without weeping, thanked Clark over and over for saving their sons. Mrs. Croft, whose Abe had been lost in the mishap, wiped away tears as she shared how difficult the adjustment to life without Abe had been for his brother Casey, but she was so thankful they had been able to see Abe again and that he had not been buried in the depths of the mine. They also were appreciative to Willie for making the proper arrangements concerning the blasting of the mine opening so there would be no further danger to other children.

Though it was difficult for them to truly express what they were feeling, they did try to make Clark understand how sorry they were that he had lost his leg. Clark assured them that in every circumstance of his life—whether good or bad—he believed with all of his heart that God knew his situation and was more than able to help him through it. He told them he was aware that there would be adjustments and some of them

147

would be difficult; but, though *he* was human, *God* was sovereign. The visitors looked a trifle uneasy at Clark's "strange talk." Marty, watching with understanding eyes, supposed it was as new to them as it had been to her when she had first joined Clark's household so many years before. Clark's face and voice held such confidence that in spite of their doubts, the people in the room could not but be sure he meant every word.

Finally Mrs. Croft dared to speak some of what she was feeling. "It was hard fer me not to have a preacher-man here fer my son's buryin'. Oh, I know I ain't rightly what you'd call a church person, but I believe in the Almighty. Can't say thet I'm on speakin' terms with 'im exactly . . . but . . . well, sometimes . . . 'specially in hard times like we jest been through . . . sometimes I jest wish I knew a little more 'bout 'im . . . "

It was Willie who spoke. "We have meetin's here together each Sunday. I know thet it ain't like being in a church, but we do read from the Word together an' sing a hymn or two. We sure would be welcomin' you to join us. Anyone is welcome at any time."

"Where ya meetin'?"

"Right here—in our home."

The woman's eyes took on a new light.

"What time ya meet?"

"Every Sunday at two o'clock."

"I dunno," spoke up the man. "It's a long way from town. By the time we got back home again, it'd be most dark."

The woman, disappointed, looked down at her lap and her clasped hands.

Clark spoke up. "Maybe the service could be moved up a bit earlier and not 'llowed to go fer too long."

The woman looked up again, her eyes hopeful.

"Well," said the man, sensing how much it meant to her, "we might try it fer a Sunday at the two o'clock time an' see how it goes."

The slight smile flickering across the woman's face said it all.

Andy's parents had taken no part in the conversation. Willie turned to them. "We'd be most happy to have ya join us, too."

The man was quick to dismiss the idea. He shook his head and shuffled his feet in an embarrassed fashion. What he mumbled was, "Don't think thet we be a-needin' thet. Our boy is jest fine now. Doc set his ankle and it's most as good as new."

Willie held his tongue. He wished to say that one did not go to church only when one had an apparent need, but now did not seem the proper time to say it. Clark said it—in a little different way, perhaps, but the message was there.

"We spend a bit of time in our service thanking the Lord as well. Perhaps you an' yer wife would like an opportunity to thank God thet He 'llowed yer boy to git out safely. Ya would be welcome to join us at any time—fer any reason."

The man nodded but remained silent.

Missie served them coffee and cake, and they went on their way, Mrs. Croft already counting the days until Sunday.

Maria and Juan came often. Juan, like a new man, had been to the city to make arrangements for setting up a proper office for the practice of medicine. He had stocked a supply cupboard with the medicines and equipment he would need. The townsfolk had coaxed him to move into a building that they would provide, but Juan wished to remain on his ranch. He did agree to be at a town office for two days of the week; the rest of the time he would work out of his own home. Glad that he had built a large house, he immediately converted one wing into an office and small examining room. He worried some, realizing that he had none of the conveniences of the city hospitals, but some cases could be sent out by train or stagecoach.

One night as they talked together, Clark noticed that the usually buoyant Juan was quiet. Maria tried to keep the conversation going, but it was easy to sense that something was troubling Juan. After asking about his new practice, the neighborhood, the ranch, the children, and still getting very little response from Juan, the group grew quiet.

Clark eventually turned once more to Juan. "I'm a wonderin', Doc, iffen I might see ya in the privacy of my room fer a few minutes," asked Clark. Juan offered his arm and Clark managed the distance with short, awkward hops.

Clark sat on his bed and caught his breath. He needed some kind of a crutch. He must get busy fashioning one. Hopping was far too difficult and drained him of what little strength he had.

"Something troubling . . . ?" began Juan, concerned.

"Yah," said Clark easily, "I'm a-thinkin' thet there is."

The doctor automatically reached for the offending limb and began to unpin the pant leg, but Clark stopped him.

"Leg's jest fine, Doc."

Juan was puzzled.

"Something else is bringing you pain?"

"Well, ya might say thet."

"And where is it hurting?"

"Well, I don't rightly know. Thet's what *I* was gonna be askin'."

Juan's puzzled frown deepened.

"Well," said Clark, watching Juan closely, "I kinda got the feelin' thet somethin' was hurtin' the doctor and he wasn't feelin' free to say anythin'."

Juan looked startled, and moved away to the window and stood looking out on the soft fall night.

"It shows that much?"

"It shows."

"I am indeed sorry. I did not mean to bring my feelings to this home, to bring sadness to those I care for."

"Anythin' thet ya care to talk about . . . or thet I could do?" asked Clark.

Juan stood in silence for several minutes and finally turned with a deep sigh and troubled eyes.

"I think that you have heard my story—at least in part. You know that I became a doctor against my father's wishes. You know too that I was responsible for my own brother's death—"

But Clark's hand stopped him. "No," he said emphatically, "thet's not the way I heard the story. Yer brother had gangrene in a bad leg; you amputated, as you had to. Yer brother chose to take his own life."

Juan waved that aside. "My father does not see it that way. He told me to leave that night and forbade me to ever return to his home again."

"I'm sorry," said Clark. "It must be very hard for you."

"It is. It is very hard. Now that I am again going to practice medicine, I wish with all of my heart that I could do so with my father's blessing." Juan hesitated, then continued. "That sounds very foolish to you, I'm sure, but—"

"Not at all. I think thet I'd be a-feelin' the same way."

"You would?"

"To be sure I would."

There was silence. Clark broke it. "What of yer mother? Is she still livin'?"

"I don't know. Perhaps that is what bothers me the most. My mother never dared to say so, but I think she was proud that I had chosen to be a doctor. When my father sent me away, my mother, for the first time in her life, dared to protest. She fell on her knees before him and pleaded that he reconsider. In the name of Mary and all the saints, she asked him to allow me to stay. 'Must I lose both my sons on the same night?' she cried. I can see her yet, and the vision haunts me. If only I knew that my mother was all right."

"Why don't ya jest go on down an' find out?"

"Return home?"

"Sure."

"But my father has not asked me to come."

Clark shrugged his shoulders.

The minutes dragged by as Juan struggled with the thought. Then Clark asked softly, "Are ya afraid?"

"Of my own father?" Juan's shock showed the insult of such a question.

"Well, I don't be knowin' the man. Have no idea what he might do."

"My father would never harm me, if that's what you are thinking."

"I'm thinkin' nothin'," responded Clark simply. "You were doin' the thinkin'."

Juan nodded his head in reluctant agreement.

"So," said Clark, "since ya have nothin' to fear, why is it a problem to go back?"

"I have not been asked," said Juan with a great deal of dignity. "To go back so would be like a stray puppy, crawling home for forgiveness and acceptance. Even my father would scorn such—"

"Ya mean it's a matter of pride?" Clark asked quietly.

Juan's head jerked up, his black eyes flashing fire.

"I understand," Clark nodded gravely. "A man does have his pride."

There was silence again. Juan began to pace the room. The air around them seemed to be heavy with unspoken ideas. Clark again dared to break the silence.

" 'Course a man can, with God's help, swaller his pride an' do what he knows he should. Iffen yer mother is livin', I'm sure thet she is hurtin' too. She has no idea iffen you're alive or dead. An' iffen yer father is still livin' an' has maybe changed his feelin's some, how would he ever be findin' ya to let ya know?"

Still Juan struggled with the issue.

"You do not know—" he began.

"No," agreed Clark, "I do not know. I'm admittin' to thet. But God does, an' I don't think thet *you're* admittin' to thet. Shore thing, I wasn't raised as you was raised, but things have been a bit tough fer me at times, too. Life can be pretty quick to take a swipe at a man. Sometimes we can't duck the blows. We jest gotta take 'em head-on. They smart a bit, to be sure. But . . . " Clark allowed his gaze to rest on his stub of a leg, "He knows all thet. He not only knows, but He cares. He doesn't ask from us thet we *understand* or even *like* what we face, but jest thet we face it like a man, an' do what we know to be right, regardless of the fact thet it goes against us at times."

"And the right thing for me as you see it?"

"I can't tell ya thet. I know thet iffen ya are troubled 'bout things as they be now, then maybe ya should do somethin' to try to straighten 'em out. I know thet mothers can pain somethin' awful, not knowing 'bout their sons. I know thet fathers can make mistakes thet they suffer fer, an' sometimes it's most difficult to be man enough to say they was wrong. Thet's all I know. Yes . . . I know another thing, as well. I know thet God can help us do the right thing—even though it seems impossible. But only you can decide what is the right thing fer you."

Juan weighed the words of the older man. At length he turned to him and extended his hand.

"I am not making any promises, except that I will think about what you have said. It is a very hard thing."

Clark took the hand and shook it firmly. "I will be prayin' thet you make the right decision," he said.

They returned to the others. There were questions in many eyes but none were asked. Maria and Juan soon declared that they must be on their way home.

Cookie came to visit Clark whenever his work would allow him a break. He usually waited until he saw Clark out on the veranda getting some fresh air or early morning sun, and then he would hobble over to ease himself to a step or a nearby chair. He seemed to feel he and Clark had much in common. One day he even dared to talk about it.

"Leg bother ya much?"

"Not bad now. Gives me a bit of a jar iffen I happen to bump it."

"Trouble with 'phantom pain'?"

"Some."

"Must be peculiar feelin'. Somethin' hurtin' thet ain't even there."

"Yah, bothers me some all right. Itches somethin' awful at times, an' ya ain't even got anythin' to scratch." Clark chuckled ruefully.

"Well, at least I don't have them problems," said Cookie.

"Yer leg still pain ya a good deal?" asked Clark.

"Sometimes." There was a moment of silence while Cookie

thought of the pain. "Not as bad lately though. Was a time I near went wild with it."

Clark nodded his head in understanding.

"How many years now?" he asked.

"I try to fergit. Guess it must be 'bout five already. No, six. Lotsa' folks said as how I'd a-been better off to have it off like you done."

"Well," Clark reminded him, "I wasn't able to do my own choosin'. Don't know's I would have really picked this way to do it, iffen I had."

"Yer leg was bad broke, Clark," Cookie assured him evenly. "I knew as soon as I seed it thet only a miracle could save it, an' seems to me we been a little short on miracles in my lifetime."

Clark smiled. "Well," he said firmly, "I ain't seen an overabundance of miracles myself, but I shore ain't doubtin' them none." Watching Cookie's expectant face carefully, Clark went on, "Guess one of the biggest miracles thet I know of is when God takes a no-good sinner and makes a saint fittin' fer heaven outa 'im. Now, thet's a real miracle, to my thinkin'. Even an earthly fella like the doc can, with some trainin' an' the right tools an' medicine, put a badly messed-up body together ag'in. But only God, through His love an' grace, can take a crushed and broken soul and restore it ag'in. Yessir, *thet's* a miracle."

Cookie scuffed the dust with the toe of his boot.

"Take me now," Clark said confidingly, "ya know what happened with me? When I first woke up to the fact thet I only had one leg, a part of me died inside. I started tellin' myself all kinds of stories 'bout bein' only half a man, an' how sad it was to be a cripple, an' how sorry I could be fer myself, an' even how God had let me down. Fer a minute, I almost had me convinced thet I had good reason to jest turn over to the wall and have a real good feelin'-sorry-fer-myself time. My body was broken—was bruised and hurtin'—an' my soul wanted to sympathize with it, see? My soul wanted to curl up an' hurt an' suffer an' become bitter an' ugly. Now, God didn't choose to do a miracle on this here leg." Clark tapped the stump lightly. "But He did a bigger an' more important miracle. He worked over the inner me—the soul of me. Thet's where I needed the miracle the most, so thet's where He applied His amazin' power. In here," said Clark, pointing to his broad chest, "in here, I don't hurt anymore."

Cookie's eyes hinted ever so slightly of unshed tears, and Clark wondered how many years Cookie had been in pain both inwardly and outwardly. He reached out a hand and gently squeezed the cowpoke's shoulder.

"We needn't fear," his voice was almost a whisper. "He's still doin' miracles."

Chapter Twenty-one

Growing

Willie returned to the range and the business of a ranch in the fall. Cattle needed to be rounded up and a few stray doggies branded. The steers for market needed to be cut and sorted from the herd and driven to the train station for shipping. Fences needed fixing and pastures had to be checked before the coming winter, besides the water holes to watch and rustlers to keep an eye out for. The warm fall days were busy from dawn till dark.

Missie still insisted on spending most of her time with her father. At times her own work suffered because of the attention she was giving Clark. The two little boys did not seem to fare too badly because they also were usually hovering closely around their grandfather. It was Willie who concerned Marty. Often when he would come in at night, tired from another busy day in the saddle, Missie was still so busy fussing over Clark that she scarcely had time to notice. Marty hoped that she was exaggerating things and tried to tuck her anxiety into the back of her mind. She tried to take care of Clark so com-

156

pletely that Missie would not feel this responsibility, but this did not ease the situation. Missie still hovered close by.

Marty then turned some of her attention to Willie, hoping to at least make him aware that he was still loved and appreciated. She of course knew instinctively that Willie wished for the attention of his wife—not his mother-in-law. Even the boys did not run to meet Willie with the same exuberance at the end of the day, for they had spent the day with a grandfather who carved them tops and fashioned whistles.

In spite of her determination to put the matter aside, Marty felt her concern grow daily. To her surprise, Clark, who was normally so sensitive to the feelings of others, did not seem to notice it. Perhaps he was just too close to the situation.

Henry came to see Clark. After a simple greeting, Henry did not sit and idly chat but came directly to the point.

"Been doin' a great deal of thinkin' lately," he said. "We really need us a church."

Clark nodded his head in agreement and looked up from the crude crutch that he was carving, having determined that it was time he did something to aid in walking.

"Good idea," said Clark.

"Seems like now would be as good a time as any to be plannin' fer it," Henry went on. "I know thet now ain't a good time at all fer ranchers. Real busy time of the year, but things will be slowin' down 'fore too long again. But we shouldn't wait fer things to slow down 'fore we git started. Thet's sorta like puttin' God last. Been thinkin' thet we really are in need of some preachin'. We read the Bible together, an' thet's good, but some of these folks need someone to explain what it's meanin'. Ya take thet there new family thet's been comin'—the Crofts—they need someone to tell them what the Word means, to show them how to accept this here truth fer themselves."

"I was thinkin' thet when ya said 'church' ya was a-meanin' a buildin'," said Clark.

"Well, I was, an' I wasn't," answered Henry. "Shore, we need a buildin', an' I think thet we could be workin' on thet real soon too. But I was also thinkin' of people an' of those who are needin' to know the truth. I think thet it's time to be givin' 'em more than we been doin'."

"Sounds good to me," responded Clark. "Ya got any plans?"

"Yah," said Henry, "been thinkin' on you."

"Me?" Clark showed surprise.

Henry did not waver. "Shore. You."

"But I don't have no Bible trainin'.'"

"Ya been studyin' it fer years, haven't ya?"

"Yah, but—"

"An' you've heard lots of preachin'?'"

"Shore."

"An ya believe the Holy Spirit can teach the truth?"

" 'Course I do."

Henry grinned. "An' ya ain't overly busy these days, are ya?"

Clark began to chuckle. "No," he said, "I shore ain't over busy. Been makin' a few tops an' whistles, an' tying a few knots, an' eatin', an' complainin', an' makin' folks run around waitin' on me. Come to think on it," he said, scratching his head with the blunt end of his knife, "seems I been powerful busy after all."

They laughed together.

"Well?" spoke Henry, when they had stopped their laughing.

"Well," responded Clark, "I need to do some thinkin' an' prayin' 'bout thet one."

"You do thet," encouraged Henry and straightened up, feeling quite confident where Clark's thinking and praying would lead him.

"Gotta git," said Henry. "The fellas will be wonderin' where their boss has disappeared to. See ya come Sunday." And he swung up into the saddle and left the yard at a canter.

Clark continued his work on his crutch but his eyes were thoughtful. In fact, he paused occasionally to wipe away a tear or two. Maybe God could turn this whole tragic accident into something good.

The group which gathered on Sunday in the large living room of the LaHaye household had again increased. With the Crofts were two other women and their children. One was the mother of Andy, the boy that Clark had rescued from the mine. The other woman, young and frightened looking, had just buried an infant son.

Four of the LaHaye cowboys sauntered in and took inconspicuous seats toward the back of the room, clearing their throats and fingering their wide-brimmed hats self-consciously as they waited for the singing to begin. The simple service was just starting when Cookie hobbled in with a rather reluctant Wong in tow. Cookie had assured Wong that this was a good place to add some new English words to his vocabulary.

Henry and his guitar led the singing, and Willie read the Scripture. After a time for prayer and another song, Willie made opportunity for anyone from the congregation to share a scripture or a thought. Henry rose to his feet. Clearing his throat, he began slowly with what he seemed to feel was a very important matter.

"Ya all know as how we been feelin' the need to git together like this Sunday by Sunday to hear the Word an' pray. Maybe ya been appreciatin' it as much as I have been, but ya still feel thet somethin' is missin' like. So much of the Word thet we read we need to learn more 'bout. Thet's why churches have 'em preachers—to explain the meanin' of the Word. Well, we ain't had us a preacher. 'Course we do have the Spirit of God as our teacher, an' I thank God fer thet.

"This here summer Missie an' Willie had the fortune of havin' Mr. and Mrs. Davis come fer a visit. It was jest to be a short visit of a couple of weeks. We all know of the tragic circumstances thet led 'em to still be here. I say 'tragic' 'cause thet's the way it seems to all of us. But I been a-thinkin'. Maybe God can make good outa even this tragedy. The Word says thet all things can work together fer our good, iffen we love God. Lately I've been seein' some good thet might come from this as well. I spoke to Mr. Davis 'bout it, an' he promised to pray 'bout it. I've asked Mr. Davis iffen he won't be our preacher-like an' explain the Word to us Sunday by Sunday. Now, he ain't a preacher, really. He's a farmer. But he knows the Word of God an' he's heard lots of preachin', an' I think thet he'd have lots of good Bible teachin' to share with us."

Faces began to turn toward Clark, and it was apparent that many people were waiting expectantly to see how he would answer Henry when the time came for a decision. Clark looked around him at the strange little congregation. He saw Missie and Willie, Henry and Melinda, and knew how much they had grown in the faith; he saw rough cowhands, unknowing but open to the knowledge of the Word; he saw the young woman from town, her sorrow showing in her eyes as she longed for some kind of comfort; he saw the Crofts, seeking for healing in their recent bereavement; he saw the family and their son whose arm still needed to be straightened; he saw Andy sitting stiffly beside his mother; he saw the De la Rosas, with the pain and the questions still lingering in Juan's eyes. Clark's heart went out to them all. He felt a strange stirring within and he knew that, with God's help, he must feed this flock. He stood up, his crutch held firmly in his hand for support, and looked around at the faces before him.

"It honors me to be asked to open God's Word with ya here. With God's help, I will try to give to ya the meanin' of the scripture read each Sunday. We can learn together."

He sat down and clapping echoed through the room. Marty was so proud and happy she wanted to put her head against Clark's shoulder and weep tears of joy.

Henry stood again, his face beaming. "We got us a preacher!" he exulted. "Now, what we gonna do 'bout a church?"

There was enthusiastic and spontaneous response to the question. Many voices began to call that they would build their own church, and some shouted suggestions about where it should be located. Henry finally got things quieted enough to speak again.

"I've been a-thinkin'," he said, "thet since there's not a church in town yet, an' this is a powerful distance fer some to travel, thet we ought to try to even things up a bit, an' put the church 'bout halfway fer everyone."

"I'm 'bout halfway!" cried Mr. Newton, jumping to his feet. "I shore would be right proud to be givin' some of my land fer a church."

Others nodded, their eyes shining; it was agreed that the church building could be located on the Newton ranch. "We'll need us timber an' materials an' a buildin' plan," said Henry. "Lots of things to be decided."

"Then let's git us a committee," someone called.

It was decided that Willie, Henry, and Mr. Newton would be the building committee. The rest of the congregation would wait for orders and do their bidding. Excitement ran so high that tongues could not slow down even when Missie served coffee and cookies. They were going to have their own church! It was a dream come true.

Chapter Twenty-two

Moving

Marty wrote another long letter home. They would not be returning to the farm until the next spring. Though Clark was daily gaining strength and was now able to stand the train trip, he was going to stay and help establish the new church by giving the people lessons from the Scriptures and encouraging them in their building project.

Marty was pleased to see the enthusiasm with which Clark greeted each new day. He spent hours poring over his well-worn Bible, and as his eyes found new truths, his lips shared them with others. He could not even wait for Sundays but spoke excitedly with anyone who was within listening distance.

Clark also was busy with other matters, thinking often of little inventions that would help him in overcoming his handicap. Daily his independence was growing. He scarcely needed help with anything anymore. He even devised a way to again ride horseback with the men or with Nathan. He moved about the ranch on his own, carrying buckets or saddles in the hand that wasn't busy with the crutch. He traveled to the garden and helped to dig the last of Missie's vegetables. He went with Nathan to gather eggs and prepared fryers for Sunday dinner. Watching him move about with confidence and assurance, Marty marvelled and rejoiced.

Missie, too, was glad to see her father up and around again. But she still could not keep from fussing over him. In her admiration for him, she chose to show her love by trying to make him comfortable whenever she came near him, by feeding him special treats from the kitchen, by entertaining him with chats and games. Marty could no longer ignore her concern. Surely Willie could not help but miss the attention that should rightly have been his.

Marty took a walk, hardly knowing how to handle her problem. Certainly Clark was loved in Missie's home. Willie had great respect for him. Missie loved him deeply, and the boys doted on their grandfather. Still, Willie's immediate family needed their own father and husband, and he needed Missie and their sons.

Marty wondered just how to discuss the problem with Clark. Would he see her concern and understand? What could they do? They were committed now to staying for the winter. And it wasn't possible to live in Missie's home and shut oneself away.

At last Marty decided that she must at least talk about the problem with Clark. If he did not see it as anything to get concerned about, then Marty too would try once again to put it from her mind.

That night after they had retired, Marty timidly broached the subject. She hoped Clark wouldn't think that she was just being foolish.

"I've been a-thinkin'," said Marty slowly. "It must be rather difficult fer Willie with us here."

"Willie?"

"Well, it wouldn't be, normally. But now, with yer accident an' all."

"I try not to cut in on Willie's time," answered Clark. "I know thet he's a very busy man. I've even found a few little ways thet I've been able to help lately."

"Oh, Willie ain't feelin' thet yer a loafer," assured Marty quickly. "I know thet. He's always tellin' me jest how special it is fer 'im to have ya here. An' he tells me too of how ya been organizin' the corrals an' fixin' up his barn."

"Yer talkin' 'bout his family, huh?"

"Ya mean—"

"I've been thinkin' on it, too. Missie fusses far too much. It's done in love, an' I 'preciate it, but it don't leave her much time fer fussin' over her husband—over the boys, too. I love 'em both dearly. But they're gittin' so's they come to me when they scratch a knee or pound a finger."

"You've noticed!" exclaimed Marty with relief.

"I've noticed. An' now thet you've noticed, it won't be near so hard fer me to make the suggestion thet I been thinkin' on."

"Suggestion?"

"Well, we can't jest up an' pull out now. They do need us to git thet there little church started. We can't leave 'em now, Marty."

Marty agreed.

"An' it don't seem too smart to be a-carryin' on here in the same household as Willie an' Missie. Two families in the same house—especially when one of 'em is the grandparents—often don't work so good."

"So?" Marty queried.

"So I think thet it's 'bout time fer a move."

"A move? Now where could we move? Yer not thinkin' of goin' into thet wild town—"

Clark stopped her with a laugh. "No, no wild town."

"Then—"

"The soddy."

"The—the *soddy*?" Marty was incredulous.

"Why not? Willie and Missie lived in it fer two winters, an' they had Nathan at the time. Surely you an' me could stand it fer one. Jest the two of us. I've been thinkin' thet it might even be fun." Marty still looked unconvinced.

"I've been checkin' it over," Clark went on enthusiastically. "The walls are sturdy, the windows in place. The roof looks

real good. Guess Willie jest had a new one put on to humor
Missie fer our comin' out here. No reason a'tall why we
couldn't be nice an' comfy fer the winter there."

Marty's initial aversion to the idea began to drain away.
She laughed softly. "Well, I never dreamed thet I'd be livin' in
a soddy. An' at my age!"

"Ya keep referrin' to yer age," said Clark. "I refuse to con-
sider myself married to an old woman, so ya jest better stop
sayin' thet."

Marty laughed again.

"Well," prompted Clark. "What 'bout the soddy? Ya
willin'? It still has the furniture—such as it is."

"Why not?" said Marty. "Think of the time thet I'll have
jest to sit an' read or sew. Not much to keepin' a soddy up."

"Then it's settled. We'll move in first thing tomarra."

"Don't ya think thet Missie might need some time to be
thinkin' on the idea?"

"She'll git used to it. Ya give her time, an' she might jest
think of all the reasons why we shouldn't."

"Maybe," agreed Marty. "All right, we'll move tomarra
then."

She kissed Clark and turned over to go to sleep. In the
darkness, a smile played around her lips. She and Clark were
going to live in a soddy! Wouldn't her friends back home think
that something else? Well, she'd have her share of experiences
to tell them, that was for sure. She could hardly wait to write a
letter back home to the children. Imagine that—she and Clark
living in a soddy!

Chapter Twenty-three

Callers

The next morning at the breakfast table, Nathan was busy shoving in Wong's muffins and making plans for himself and his grandfather for the day.

"An' we can ride over to the big hill an' look right over the range to where all the hands will be drivin' the cattle. We can see 'em start off on the trail drive to the town market. An'—"

"Whoa, cowboy," said Clark. "Thet shore sounds like a lot of fun all right, but I'm afraid thet I can't be runnin' off today. Fact is, I was thinkin' of askin' fer yer help today."

Nathan looked at his grandfather with surprise but quickly shifted his plans. "Sure, Grandpa. I'll help ya."

Josiah cut in. "Me help G'an'pa."

"You're too little," Nathan broke in, but Clark was quick to reassure the younger boy. "Shore ya can help. We gonna need all the hands thet we can git."

Josiah beamed at being included.

"What're you up to?" asked Missie, her curiosity overcoming her.

"Yer ma and me decided to move today."

"Move?"

"Yep."

"Stop your joshin'," said Missie.

"Not joshin'. Never been more serious."

"Then what do you mean, 'move'?"

"Well, we decided thet it might be kinda fun to spend a winter in the soddy."

"You *are* joshin'!" Missie could not believe that Clark was serious.

"No, I'm not."

"Why would you ever do that?"

"Why not? The soddy is snug and warm and big enough fer the two of us. It would be an adventure to talk about when we git back home."

"Oh, Pa," said Missie in exasperation. "Don't talk about anything so silly."

"Little girl," said Clark firmly, "It's not silly and I really am serious 'bout this."

Missie turned to Marty. "Tell me he's only teasin'."

"No," said Marty matter-of-factly. "He's not. We talked it all over last night. We decided thet it would be better fer all of us if we lived separate fer the winter."

Missie arose from her chair, her face white and set.

"I don't understand one word of what you're sayin'," she said. "Iffen you're serious, I'd like to know why. Haven't we been carin' for you—?"

Clark interrupted her. "My dear," he said gently, "ya shore as the world have been doin' everythin' fer me—an fer yer ma. An' we 'preciate it—more'n we ever could say. But now thet I'm gittin' about an' am able to sorta care fer myself some, well, yer ma an' me think thet it's 'bout time thet yer family had ya back ag'in—all to themselves."

Willie's eyes widened, then he lowered his gaze. Marty knew that he would say nothing, but she also knew that he had realized they understood well the situation in his home.

"That's silly," fumed Missie. "My family has had me all along. Never have I been more'n a few feet away from any of them. Why, they always knew right where to find me. We've loved havin' you here. After all, it was because you came to see us that you lost that leg."

Clark interrupted. "Missie, I don't want to ever hear ya say thet I lost my leg because I came here. It coulda happened at home jest as well as here. The place has nothin' to do with it, an' I never want ya to feel any kind of guilt thet the accident happened because I was here."

Missie lowered her eyes and brushed aside Clark's comment. "Well," she said, "I won't feel guilt—I promise—but I still don't understand your wantin' to move on out. We love to have you here. Before we know it, the winter will be over an' you'll be off home again. We want you here as much as possible. Tell 'em, Willie," she implored her husband. But Willie merely continued eating his scrambled eggs and muffins.

"Tell 'em, Willie," Missie said again.

Willie swallowed and looked from one to the other. It was apparent that he did not wish to be involved in the discussion. Clark spoke up before Willie was obliged to answer for himself.

"We know thet our son-in-law would never suggest thet we leave his home an' his table. We really want to do it, Missie, not because we are not welcome here, but because we feel thet it would be good fer all of us. We'll be right nearby and can come in fer coffee whenever we need a stroll. Yer ma will be over often to borrow cups of sugar and talk 'girl talk.' The boys can come an' visit us in the soddy." Clark winked. "It could be jest a heap of fun. Marty an' I have never lived all by ourselves, ya know."

"An' nothin' that I can say will make you change your mind?" Missie said, in one last effort at persuasion.

" 'Fraid not. Iffen the winter gits too tough an' we begin to get cold, we might come crawlin' back a-beggin' to be 'llowed in," said Clark, in an effort to keep things light.

"I'll let ya in, Grandpa," assured Nathan, and everyone began to laugh.

"I'll let ya in, G'an'pa," echoed Josiah, not wanting to be outdone.

Missie moved for the coffeepot. "Well, if you are determined to do it, I guess I can't stop you, but I still don't like it."

"Look, honey," said Marty, understanding how the girl felt, "if we didn't think thet it is fer the best, we wouldn't do it. Honest! Jest give it a chance, will ya, Missie? Iffen it doesn't seem to be workin' fer the best of all concerned, we'll move back in here. Please?"

Missie brightened some and leaned over to kiss Marty on her forehead.

"I'm sorry. It just took me off-guard like." She managed a smile. "Iffen you're sure that it's what you want, my soddy is all yours. But I'm warnin' you, Mama, it can get awful cramped on a winter's day."

Marty laughed. "Well, I have an advantage thet you didn't have, my dear."

"Meanin'?" asked Missie.

"You," said Marty. "Iffen I git to feelin' cramped, I can jest bundle up an' make a dash fer yer big, beautiful home. You didn't have a big house nor a daughter nearby, so ya jest had to sit tight."

Missie smiled again. "Well, I hope that you feel cramped real often," she said. "Then you'll visit me lots."

Clark put down his empty cup. "Well, fellas," he said to the boys, "guess we'd better git started with this here move."

The boys scrambled down and led the way to the bedroom that had been known as Grandpa and Grandma's for the last few months. Clark followed, his crutch beating a rhythmic tatoo behind them.

"I'll see what I can find for rugs an' blankets," offered Missie. "You'll need some decent dishes, too. Those in the soddy are in bad shape."

"Now, don't ya fuss none," Marty warned her daughter, but she knew that she might as well bid the sun not to shine. Missie was sure to fuss. Marty just shrugged her shoulders. Perhaps in the fussing Missie would find some fun. She followed Missie out, determined to make a real adventure for them all on this moving day.

The nights were cooler now, and the wood fire in the old

cookstove made the snug little soddy cozy and warm. Clark had encouraged Marty to visit Missie often during the first few days after their move, to assure her that indeed they had not forsaken her. Marty also invited Missie down to the soddy for afternoon tea; and Missie's many memories of the small shack gave her parents a new understanding of their daughter's first years in the West. She told of her first shocking sight of the small, grass-covered mound that was to be her home, and her horror at seeing from inside the dirt roof and dirt floor, and her feeling of fear as she laid Nathan on the bed lest the chunks of earth come tumbling down on top of the wee baby. She described their first Christmas and the cowboys sitting almost toe-to-toe, enjoying a simple Christmas dinner. She told of Cookie holding the baby Nathan and helping him to breathe freely again when he had the croup. She talked about her first visit from Maria, her difficulty in drying her wash, her cooped-up feelings; but all the time she talked there was nostalgia in her voice, and her deep affection for the old sod shack showed. Marty even began to wonder if Missie might be envying their chance to live in the little soddy!

The boys loved to come, and Marty and Clark found themselves listen.ng for their knock on the door and the two little voices calling, "Grandpa!" "G'am'ma!" They would pester Clark as he tried to study for the Sunday lessons. They coaxed to be able to add fuel to the fire. They wanted to roll on the bed, scratch marks in the dirt floor, and have their meals at the small table. They brought garden vegetables, fresh eggs, or milk from their mother. They even brought treats from Wong's kitchen.

Clark and Marty enjoyed them but always made sure they were home to greet their father when he returned at the end of the day.

Life finally had settled into a warm, comfortable, wholesome routine for all of them. Marty was thankful that Clark had proposed the move, feeling that it truly was better for all concerned. Willie looked less tense, more relaxed and happy, as well. He had needed to be master in his own home again. Even Missie took on a new glow. The past months had drained all of them, but now it was time for life to return to normal once more.

Marty sat in front of the soddy, knitting and soaking in the late fall sun; Clark came around the corner, expertly managing his crutch and a pail of spring water. He set the pail down and sank into a chair beside Marty, wiping his brow.

His chuckle brought Marty's head up. *Now what is he findin' so funny?* she asked herself and then repeated it to Clark.

"Nothin's funny, really. Jest thinkin' thet God really *does* make 'all things work together fer good.' "

"Meanin'?"

"This here leg—the one thet I ain't got no more. Ya noticin' which one is missin'?"

"Yah, the left one."

"It's the left one—but more'n thet. Look, it frees up my right hand when I'm a doin'. See, I use the crutch in the left. Not only thet, but thet there left one is the one thet I chopped into thet winter takin' out logs. Remember?"

Marty wondered how he thought she could forget. She still went weak and sick inside when she thought of Clark's return to the house with his pale face and blood-drenched foot.

"I remember," she said, her voice tight.

"Well, thet's the foot thet's gone. Thet rascal has kept me awake more'n one night—'specially when the weather's 'bout to change."

"You never mentioned thet before."

"Weren't no reason to. Guess it won't keep me awake again though."

Clark chuckled again. Marty couldn't quite bring herself to join him, but she smiled at this strong, patient man of hers who saw God's hand in all the circumstances of his life.

Clark had a visit from Juan. It had been three weeks since they had seen the De la Rosas. They had been informed that Juan and Maria had gone away and assumed that Juan was still gathering equipment and supplies for his medical practice. He greeted Clark now with a firm handshake and clear eyes. Marty sensed that he wanted to talk to Clark in private and left the two of them alone over steaming cups of coffee.

"Well, after much prayer and struggle," began Juan immediately, "I did as you recommended."

"You have been home?"

"I have been home," Juan said with deep feeling.

"I'm glad," said Clark. "An' how did yer pa receive you?"

Juan's eyes clouded for a moment. "My father, I am sorry to say, was not there to greet me. He died seven months ago."

"I'm sorry," Clark said with sincerity.

"I am sorry, too. I should have gone sooner. I should not have let stubborn pride keep me away."

"An' yer mother?"

"My mother welcomed me with outstretched arms."

Clark smiled. "I'm sure she did."

"My father had died and left my mother all alone. Daily she prayed that if her son Juan was still living he would come back to her. Because of my foolishness, it took a long time for my mother's prayers to be answered."

"We are all foolish at times," Clark reminded him.

Juan went on. "My mother could scarcely believe her eyes when I walked into her room. She had failed much. She did not eat well or care for herself since my father died. When she saw me, she wept long for joy. Then she told me how my father had pined after sending me away. He tried for many months to find me—to ask for my forgiveness—but there was no trace of where I had gone. Before he died, he had my mother promise that she would keep trying. She did. She sent out men and offered rewards, but she could not find me."

Juan stopped to wipe a hand across his eyes. "I caused them much hurt," he murmured.

"Ya didn't know."

"No, I didn't know. I was too busy nursing hurts of my own. . . . My mother was so happy to hear that I am a doctor again. I would like you to meet her."

"I'd love to meet her. Maybe someday—"

"Not someday. Now."

"Ya mean—?"

"She's here. I left her up at the house having tea with Missie and Maria. She wants very much to meet the man who sent her son home to her."

"But I . . . I didn't do thet. Ya went on yer own. It was yer decision."

"Yes, you let me make the decision. You left me my dignity. But you knew when you talked to me how I would have to decide." Juan smiled.

"I'd love to meet yer mama," said Clark, picking up his crude crutch.

"An' I have something for you," said Juan, returning to the door and reaching outside for a carefully fashioned crutch with a padded arm bar. "They can make very good crutches in the city," he added.

Clark took the new crutch and handled it carefully, looking over every angle and the total length of it.

"It's a dandy," he grinned. "An' I thank ya."

Clark, with his new "store-bought" crutch, and Juan went to the house together. Juan explained as they walked, "My mother had no desire to live alone on the rancho. As I did not wish to return to ranching in that area, we decided to sell the ranch to the man who has run it for my father. Mother is insisting on using much of the money from the sale for my medical practice. She wants us to have good equipment for those who need help. She is going to live with us. We are all so happy. Maria can't remember having a mother. Hers died when she was a very young girl. We are all very happy, Mr. Clark, and we thank you."

Señora De la Rosa was a delicate, dark woman with flashing eyes and a quick smile. In spite of her years and the intense sorrow in her past, she still had a youthful spirit and vibrant outlook on life. Clark and Marty liked her immediately.

"Mama has said that we shall all come to service together," said Maria. "When God works to answer her prayers through people who worship—even though they worship in a different way than she is used to—they must have the approval of God, she says. And so God would also surely approve of us worshiping together with them. So we shall be here next

Sunday—and all the Sundays—and we will be glad to help in the building of the new church."

The prayer time together before the De la Rosas left for home was full of fervent thanksgiving to God.

Chapter Twenty-four

Winter

Nathan celebrated his sixth birthday—a big event for him at any time, but even more important on this occasion because his grandparents were there to help in the merrymaking. The Kleins and De la Rosas also came for the event, and the house rang with laughter and chatter.

Josiah got a full share of the attention on the occasion; he came in from the kitchen bundled up in one of Wong's big white aprons and looking like a huge cocoon. Everyone had a good laugh, and Joey was pleased with the response.

Nathan had insisted that he wanted a crutch "jest like Grandpa's" for his birthday and could not understand the objections to getting him one. He wished to imitate his grandfather in every way, and he felt that the use of a crutch—even though he did plan to keep his leg—would be one more thing that he could share with the man whom he loved so dearly. Missie was horrified at the very thought of such a thing, fearing that Nathan toting about a crutch might be tempting fate. She tried to talk Nathan out of it, promising him all kinds of things in its place. Nathan still wanted one. Clark finally had a man-to-man talk with the boy, and Nathan came away from the talk happy to be able to walk on two good legs "like his pa."

Willie was pleased with the profit from the fall cattle sale, and he and Missie left by train for a larger city to do some shopping. Clark and Marty cared for the two boys while the LaHayes were gone.

The shipment of furnishings eventually arrived, and Missie now had a new dining room—splendid in its dark wood furniture, thick rug and rich draperies. Marty complimented Missie many times on her excellent taste, but Missie laughed and replied that anyone had good taste as long as he had good money.

Missie, too, had a birthday. Marty thoroughly enjoyed the chance to make the cake and prepare the birthday dinner after the number of years they had been apart on Missie's birthday. All of the ranch hands were invited for the meal. The large family dining room was almost as crowded as the little soddy had been many Christmases ago. But Missie loved it, and the cowboys all seemed to appreciate it, too.

The winter's first storm moved in without warning. Marty awoke to hear the wind howling around the little soddy. Clark was already up and reading his Bible at the small table while the fire sent out comforting waves of heat, even though the wind tried to tear away its warmth.

Marty snuggled down under the covers again and thought about how fortunate they were. Winter might be here with all of its fury, but they were snug and warm and dry. Marty did not put off getting up for long; Clark had coffee perking, and the smell of it quickly drove away her sleepiness and enticed her from the bed. She crawled forth rather hesitantly but the howling wind had no power in their warm shelter.

"My, thet coffee be smellin' good! I think thet ya purposely made it jest to tempt me from the bed," she said, slipping her arms around Clark's shoulders and giving him a kiss on the cheek.

"Ya hear thet wind?" asked Clark. "Sounds like we're gonna find out all 'bout a western winter."

"Guess we will at thet," said Marty, "but ya know, it ain't scarin' me none."

Clark merely smiled.

"Whatcha doin'?" asked Marty.

"Well, Henry figures thet when the storms strike on Sundays the folks from any distance won't be able to make it here fer the service. So we talked it over an' decided to make 'em up some lesson materials so thet they might do their own readin' at home."

"Thet's a good idea!" Marty responded.

"At least this be helpin' 'em to feel a part of the group even iffen they can't git here. They'll be studyin' the same portion of the Word as the rest of us."

"Thet's nice," Marty said again.

"But I've been at this fer what seems ages already, an' I shore could do with breakfast. I was jest sittin' here a-thinkin' this shore is the kind of a mornin' thet I could use a nice big stack of pancakes."

Marty laughed and went to get dressed so that she could make Clark his pancakes.

The winter weather continued as it had begun. The storms moved in and out of the area. As predicted, the Sunday crowd at the LaHayes' diminished. Henry saw to it that the other members of the little congregation received Clark's Sunday lesson materials.

The church building committee worked hard at drawing plans and arranging for the materials for spring building. All the members of the group were anxious to get into their own little church. Juan's mother sent away to the city and ordered a bell for the spire. She felt that a church of God should have a bell with which to call together the worshipers.

Donations for materials or for labor came in from many of the neighbors. Willie and Henry were sure that when a building was finally in evidence, the Sunday attendance would increase sharply.

Cookie still dropped in to see Clark often. Marty was sure that he waited until he saw her heading for Missie's for a chat over a cup of tea, and then he would hobble off to have a cup of coffee with Clark in her absence. Clark did not discuss with her much of their conversation—Marty knew that Clark honored Cookie's desire for confidence; yet Marty realized that the old cowboy was deeply troubled about his past life and its effect on his future. Marty wanted to hasten "the awakening" and say outright to Cookie, "So yer a sinner an' ya realize thet yer bad deeds can keep ya from heaven. I was a sinner, too. But one needn't stay in thet state. Christ Jesus came so thet every person could be forgiven and restored to all that God intended when He created us. All ya need do, Cookie, is to accept the gift of life that He offers to ya. It's jest thet simple. Nothin' to it at all. No need to be a-frettin' an' a-stewin' over whether it be a good idea or a bad idea. Common sense tells ya thet ya can't lose on such a deal. Jest do it an' git it taken care of."

Clark was far more patient with the man and explained carefully what Scripture had to say about the original fall into sin and selfishness, man's need of a Savior, and God's solution to this need. Cookie was gradually realizing his need and understanding what Christ had done for him. Clark felt confident that when Cookie made his decision, there would be no turning back. Still, Marty inwardly chafed, wishing it wouldn't take him so long.

Scottie, too, was on the Davises' prayer list. They liked and respected the foreman, and they wished to see him make his peace with God. Scottie came to the Sunday services whenever he was free to do so, but he did not seem to feel any need of a change in his life.

Lane, the one who had helped Doc De la Rosa with the surgery, was growing spiritually. Daily he sought out Clark or Willie for the answer to some question that he found as he read the Word. He not only read the Bible, but he endeavored to live daily by its commands and concepts. Lane could never be accused of being a hypocrite. Even the bitter Smith began to show a grudging respect for Lane and one day admitted to Jake, "Don't hold much to religion. Always figured thet it was fer women an' kids an' men who couldn't stand on their own feet; but iffen I was ever to git religion, I'd want the kind thet Lane got."

Jake looked skeptical. "Didn't know there was more'n one kind," he drawled.

"Ya didn't? Then ya ain't been watchin' Lane lately."

"So where did Lane git his special brand?" sneered Jake.

"Reckon he got it from the same place thet the boss an' his pa-in-law got theirs. It seems to be made of the same stuff."

Jake thought of Willie and his steadiness even through the tough times, his fairness with his men, and his concern for his community. He also thought of Clark and his acceptance of his handicap, and he murmured under his breath, "Yah, reckon it is." Then he turned to Smith. "So, iffen they are able to pass it on an' are so anxious to share it, what's stoppin' ya from gittin' yerself some?"

Smith did not answer. He just scowled and rode away.

Chapter Twenty-five

Christmas

Christmastime arrived, and Marty's thoughts were often on her family at home, even as her thoughts had been on Missie in the Christmases that they had been separated. Kate was there to help Ellie make a Christmas for the family on the farm, and the last letter had stated that Nandry's and Clae's families would both be home for Christmas as well, even though Clark and Marty would not be there. Soon after the new year, Joe and Clae and little Esther would be leaving for the city where Joe would finally have his opportunity to get his seminary training. Marty wished she would be there to tell them good-bye, but it brought a measure of joy to her heart to know that they would be in the very city where Luke eventually would be going to take his medical training. It would not be nearly so hard to let him go knowing that Clae and Joe would be there to welcome him.

Even so, Marty thought much of her other family as she made her little preparations for the Christmas with the family in the West.

Wong and Cookie combined their efforts to prepare a Christmas feast for all of the members of the ranch family. It was bound to be a sumptuous affair, and everyone—old and young alike—were anticipating the occasion. Marty supposed that they would all eat more than they really needed.

Nathan and Josiah especially had worked themselves up into a fever of excitement. Nathan knew of Christmases past and the thrill of receiving gifts. Josiah was too young to remember other Christmases, but he was willing to take his big brother's word for what would happen.

Marty had busily knitted mittens, socks and scarves for the two boys, and Clark had been carefully fashioning a snow sled. "Shore enough," he told Marty, "with all them hills around, there must be one that a sled would work good on." Marty agreed. Even though they would be many days' journey away from the rest of their family, they were happy to be able to spend this Christmas with Missie, Willie, and the boys.

On Christmas Eve, Marty finished the last of her Christmas presents, and they bundled up their gifts and themselves and went out into the starlit winter night through the snow for the short trip to Missie's house. They had planned an evening of games, Christmas carols, and popcorn over the log fire. The gifts would not be exchanged until the next morning.

Nathan was the one to answer their knock. He squealed with delight, and Josiah was just behind him to echo his joy.

"Hi, Grandpa! Hi, Grandma! Come in. We're havin' Christmas," called Nathan.

"Ch'is'mas," echoed Josiah and pulled them in by the hands.

The evening was full of love and joy. They chatted and ate and played games and sang amid laughter and lighthearted banter. They shared their memories of other Christmases; Nathan loved the stories, but Josiah's heavy lids kept drooping as he fought to stay awake.

Finally Missie rose reluctantly to put the two children to bed. Nathan certainly was not anxious to go, afraid that he might miss something. Missie assured him everything would be there for him to see and share in the morning.

When the children were settled and the grownups were having coffee and slices of Wong's Christmas cake made from one of Marty's recipes, Missie, her cheeks aglow and her eyes alight, shared her secret.

"Yer to be grandparents again in July," she said. "We're gonna have another little one."

"Oh, thet's wonderful!" stated Marty, hugging her girl close. "But, my, I wish thet it would be sooner! We should be off home long 'fore then, an' it will be so hard to leave without seein' him—or her."

"I'm hopin' fer a girl this time," admitted Missie. "But a boy would be all right too. Willie's always needin' lots of cowboys on the ranch." They laughed together, and Willie looked pleased.

They talked further about their hopes and dreams concerning the new baby. Marty commented about how thankful she was that Dr. De la Rosa would be there for the birthing. And perhaps by then he would also have his little surgery all ready for use.

Clark and Marty, arm in arm, returned with happy steps and joyful hearts over the snow-packed path back to the little soddy. They were just about to enter when Cookie appeared, hobbling hurriedly toward the bunkhouse from the cookshack, a small lantern swinging by his side. Marty assumed he must be going to meet with the cowboys for their own Christmas celebration, but Clark noted an urgency to Cookie's steps.

"Somethin' wrong?" he called to Cookie.

Cookie hesitated. "No, nothin' wrong, really. Least not fer you to concern yerselves with. Scottie jest came ridin' in with some stray cowpoke thet he found out there on the range someplace. Fella's in pretty bad shape. Looks like he ain't e't in a week, an' the weather's kinda on the cold side to be a-sittin' out under a rock outcroppin'. Lane, he went over to see what the doc would advise fer his frostbite."

Cookie was about to move on, but Clark called to him.

"I'll join ya. Don't s'pose there be much thet I can do, but I'll take a look-see."

He turned to Marty and spoke softly, "Ya go on in out of

this cold to bed. I'll jest be a few minutes an' then I'll be in to join ya. Ya might want to check on the fire ag'in 'fore ya turn in."

Then Clark deftly hopped along after Cookie, his crutch making strange tracks in the fresh snow.

The cowboys had put the unfortunate man to bed, Lane directing them to his bunk before he left for the doctor's. Smithie was using the only medicine that he was acquainted with—a shot of whiskey. The man was sputtering and fussing, so Clark knew he was at least alive.

"Where'd ya find 'im?"

"Scottie found him someplace out there. He didn't even have a horse. Said it had died. He was walkin' somewhere—who knows where—an' the bad weather caught him. He tried to hole up in a sheltered spot and wait out the wind. He coulda been there till spring and not had the wind stop none."

Clark smiled in spite of his concern. "Is he in bad shape?"

"Don't know yet. He has some frostbite fer sure, an' he's thin as a rattler. 'Bout as mean as one, too, I'm a-thinkin'. All he can do is cuss an' namecall. Don't seem to 'preciate much the trouble thet Scottie took fer 'im."

Clark moved nearer to the bed.

The man before him was heavily bearded and his eyes were only dark holes in his head. Bedraggled and dirty, he looked as though he hadn't had a meal for weeks. Yet something about him was vaguely familiar.

Clark motioned for them to move the lantern in closer, the result being a gruff complaint and a curse from the stranger. Clark looked steadily into the thin, shadowed face and finally was sure.

"Jedd," he said, shaking his head in unbelief. "Jedd Larson."

Chapter Twenty-six

Jedd

The sick man stirred slightly and mumbled something incoherent. All other eyes in the room turned on Clark.

"Ya know this man?" asked Scottie.

"It's Jedd Larson, there's shore no mistakin' thet; but he shore do look in bad shape. Last I seed 'im he was still young and strong—and a mite on the stubborn side. Marty an' me raised his two girls—though it's hard fer us to remember at times thet they ain't really our own. We think of 'em as such."

"Well, I'll be a—" expostulated Cookie, though he was not allowed to finish his statement, for the ill man began to toss and call out in his delirium. Clark leaned over him in an effort to understand what the man was saying. He straightened as he caught the one word that was repeated over and over. Jedd was saying, "Tina."

"Understand 'im?" asked Cookie.

"He's askin' fer his wife. She's been gone fer a number of years now. Can't say thet Jedd treated her too kindly whilst she was here. Maybe he's regrettin' it now."

Clark reached out a hand and felt Jedd's brow, hot with

fever. He leaned over the man and spoke his name softly. There was no response. Clark knelt down beside the bed and took the man's hand in his. He began to talk to Jedd. The cowboys gradually moved back from the bed to allow the two men a degree of privacy.

"Jedd," Clark said clearly, "Jedd, this is Clark. Clark Davis, yer neighbor. Remember me, Jedd? Clark Davis. Clark and Marty. Ya left yer girls with us, Jedd, when ya decided to go west. Tina wanted 'em to have schoolin'. Tina asked Marty to give the girls a chance, Jedd. Remember? They are fine girls, Jedd, yer Nandry an' Clae. You'd be mighty proud of 'em. Both of 'em married. Nandry has a little family of four. An' Clae's got a little girl. Yer a grandpa, Jedd. A grandpa five times over. You'd be proud of yer grandkids, too, could ya see 'em."

The man was not responding. He stared off into space and now and then mumbled or cursed as the warmth of the room increased the pain in his frostbitten limbs. Clark continued to speak to him, rubbing his hand as he spoke, careful not to touch the frostbitten fingers.

"Jedd, Nandry and Clae still worry 'bout ya. Still pray fer ya daily. They want ya back, Jedd. They want to share with ya their love, their family, their God. Remember, Jedd? Tina found peace with God before she died. Well, yer girls are servin' their mother's God, too, Jedd. There's nothin' thet they would like better then fer you to know God, too. Ya hear me, Jedd? Yer girls love ya. Nandry an' Clae—they love ya. Tina loved ya, an' God loves ya too, Jedd.

"Ya gotta keep fightin', man," Clark continued, speaking softly but with urgency. "Ya can't jest go an' give up now. Hang in there, Jedd."

It seemed to the cowboys in the room that there was hardly a pause in the low murmur of Clark's voice until Lane and the doctor arrived. Dr. De la Rosa examined Jedd carefully and gave him some medication. He shook his head as he turned to Clark and the waiting ranch hands.

"He is in bad shape. He was not well even before he was caught in the storm."

"Will he make it?" asked Clark.

"I do not know."

"Please, Doc," said Clark, "iffen there is anything at all thet ya can be doin' fer 'im—anything to bring him through—I'll stand the bill. This here is the father of two girls thet Marty an' me raised as our own. He's been bullheaded and stubborn, thoughtless and sometimes cruel, but his girls love 'im. Iffen only Jedd can live long enough fer someone to tell 'im of God's love an' fergiveness. Thet would mean so much to his girls—to us. Ya think thet ya can bring him 'round, Doc? I jest can't bear the thought of 'im dyin' without my bein' able to talk with him about his girls and about God's love for 'im."

Dr. De la Rosa looked very solemn. "I can only try," he said. "You pray that God might work a miracle."

Dr. De la Rosa undoubtedly thought that Clark would go to his little soddy and kneel in prayer, but Clark saw the need as imminent. He immediately knelt beside the bed on which Jedd lay and began to pray fervently for a miracle. Around him feet shuffled as cowboys, uncertain of what to do, shifted position. Lane knew. He crossed to his bunk and knelt down beside Clark, joining him in his prayer.

"Dear God," began Clark, "Ya know this here man before us. He's been sinful, God, but so have we all. He's made some bad judgments, but so have we. He needs Ya, Lord, just as we all do. He has never recognized Ya as God an' Savior, an' he needs thet chance, Lord. He can't hear or respond in his present condition, so we need Ya to do a miracle, Lord, an' help the doc to bring him 'round so thet we can talk with him and read Yer Word so thet he might have thet chance to decide fer hisself. We are askin' this, Lord, in the name of Jesus, Yer Son, who died thet each one of us—includin' Jedd here—could have life eternal. Thank ya, Lord, for hearin' the prayer of those of us who bow before Ya. Amen."

Clark stood up, adjusting his crutch to support himself. The man before him still lay unconscious. Lane reached out and touched the whiskered cheek. Then he turned to the doctor.

"What's next, Doc?"

Juan looked back at the man on the bed. "I think I should

take him to my home. I can put him on the cot in the office."

All eyes looked at the doctor, questioning.

The doctor continued. "He is going to need much care. We can watch him there. It will give my mother the feeling to be needed. She wishes to do something for someone, and this will be her chance. If I am able to help this man . . ." Juan hesitated, then continued. "I think that it is too late to save many of his fingers and toes. Perhaps he will lose them all."

It was sobering news. Clark noticed some of the hands in the room unconsciously curl up into fists as though defying fate to try to take their own.

Lane moved first. "Ya want me to git a team?" he asked the doctor.

"Yes. Put lots of hay in the bottom of a wagon. We'll need to make him a bed."

For the second time that Christmas Eve, Lane made a trip to the doctor's, this time driving the team that carried a critically ill man. His saddle horse tied to the rear, Dr. De la Rosa rode in the wagon with them, watching Jedd to be sure he stayed well covered in the bitter winter wind.

Clark returned to the little soddy and found that Marty had not gone to bed.

"I've been a-frettin' an' thinkin' all kinds of things," she said.

"You'll never believe this," said Clark, "but thet man Scottie brought in off the range is Jedd Larson."

"Jedd?"

"Shore ain't in very good shape."

"Oh, Clark. Did ya tell 'im 'bout his girls? Did he say—"

"Jedd didn't say much 'ceptin' a few cuss words, Marty. He is plumb outa his head. No, thet's not right. He did say one thing. Over an' over. He said 'Tina.' "

"Tina . . . Then he remembers."

"Somehow thet one name gave me hope, Marty. Somehow it helped me to believe this wasn't jest fate thet sent Jedd this way, but God givin' him thet chance to find *Him*."

"Oh, Clark, I pray thet it might be so," said Marty, the tears filling her eyes.

"If only I could have talked to him—made him understand me somehow."

"Can I see 'im?" asked Marty.

"He's gone."

"Gone? But how could—"

"Lane went fer Dr. De la Rosa, an' the doc decided when he checked Jedd out thet it would be better fer 'im to have Jedd at his house so he could watch over 'im. Lane took 'im on over in the wagon. They left jest a few minutes ago."

"Oh, Clark. I hope he makes it. I hope thet ya have a chance to talk to him. Was he really bad, Clark?"

Clark nodded his head solemnly.

"Oh, Clark!" cried Marty again. "Let's pray." Once again they knelt beside the bed.

Chapter Twenty-seven

Christmas Day

In spite of anxiety over Jedd, Christmas Day was a time of thanksgiving and joy. With two small boys in the house, it was impossible not to feel excitement and pleasure concerning Christmas. Even though they had retired late the evening before and had had difficulty getting to sleep, Clark and Marty were up early and over in the big house. Nathan and Josiah, already up and filling the house with cries of happiness as they looked at the gifts which had arrived sometime during the night, were not very interested in their breakfast that day.

Nathan was thrilled with the sled that Clark had made and begged to go out and try it even before he had eaten. Clark laughed and promised the boys he would take them out on the sled just as soon as their mother approved. Missie, smiling, shrugged her shoulders helplessly.

Nathan's favorite gift from his parents was a new halter for Spider, his pony. Willie finally gave into his pleadings and told him they would go to the barn and be sure that the halter fit. Nathan soon reappeared, bundled to his eyebrows with

Marty's gift of socks, mittens and carelessly-looped scarf. Willie laughed at the sight that the boy made.

"Ya shore enough look well cared fer weather-wise, 'ceptin' fer yer feet. Ain't ya plannin' to wear any boots?"

"They won't go over my big socks," replied Nathan, which brought more laughs.

Josiah soon rounded the corner too. He was still in his nightclothes and over them he too had looped his long scarf. One eye was hidden and he peeked out from the other one, his head tipped to give him better vision. His mittens had been pulled on the wrong hands, and the empty thumbs stuck out to the side like two misplaced horns. The socks, partly on but mostly off, gave Josiah the appearance of having duck feet. He waddled forward, pleased with himself and ready to join his brother and pa for the trip to the barn. Now Willie really howled. He led the two boys back to their room, properly dressed Josiah and helped Nathan to find socks and boots that worked together. Then, with the small Josiah on his shoulders and Nathan trudging along at his side with the cherished new halter, Clark joined them and they all started out for the barn.

"They do make some sight, don't they?" said Missie at the window, a lump in her throat.

"Don't know how many times I've stood at my window an' watched yer pa an' his sons crossin' the yard," Marty responded. "Iffen I had no other reason to love yer pa than thet single one—the seein' of his carin' fer his young'uns—thet one would be enough to make me love him as long as God grants me breath," she continued softly.

They turned back to the preparations for the day. There was much to be done, for Christmas dinner for all of the hands had become a tradition on the LaHaye ranch. Though busy and going many different directions, on Christmas Day they took the time to all eat together and share the Christmas story.

That morning around the breakfast table the discussion often had been directed to the wonder of Jedd Larson turning up on the LaHaye spread. They had not heard of Jedd since he had left his farm back home and headed west so many years ago. Marty wished there was some way she could share with Clae and Nandry the exciting news, and then she sobered. If Jedd did not make it through this Christmas Day, the news they would have to share with their girls would be bad news, not good news. Again and again through the day Marty prayed.

After the trip to the barn, as promised, Clark took the bundled-up boys for a sled ride.

At first it was difficult for him to pull the sled with the two small passengers up the nearby slope, but eventually he found that his crutch, jammed into the snow, made a good replacement for the limb he did not have.

The boys squealed with delight as Clark shoved them off and they made the short, swift trip down the hill. This time, Nathan pulled the sled back up the hill, but it was hard for little Josiah to make the climb on his own. Clark went to meet him and carried him up the hill piggyback. Again and again they sped down the hill and made their slow and awkward climb back up. At last, exhausted but happy, they agreed to head back to the house and get warmed up.

"We'll have to do this ag'in, huh, Grandpa?" said Nathan.

" 'G'in," echoed his little brother.

"Shore will," said Clark, who had enjoyed it almost as much as the boys.

"After dinner?" asked Nathan.

"Well, I dunno 'bout thet. I think thet yer pa an' ma might have some of their own plans fer after dinner."

"After thet then?"

"We'll see," laughed Clark. "We'll see."

About one o'clock the cowboys began to arrive, kicking the snow from their boots and slapping their wide-brimmed hats against their sides. They laughed and joked as they filed in. Marty stood back in amazement as they stopped in the large entry and removed their boots and lined them up neatly against the wall, not wishing to damage Missie's fine rugs. Marty had been west only for a short while, but already she understood how important boots were to the ranch hands, how important it was not to be caught with your boots off. They looked embarrassed and ill at ease as they stood looking down at their stockinged feet. Marty noticed that some of the socks had holes in them and wondered if she would dare offer to darn them. She said nothing now but went to the kitchen to find a worn towel. One by one she picked up the boots and carefully wiped away all traces of water or dirt. Then she handed them, pair by pair, back to the owners. The cowboys slipped back into the boots with warm grins and eloquent nods of thanks. They were now all ready for the meal filling the air with delightful aromas as Wong carried dish after dish to the large dining room.

Before the meal, Willie, as the head of the home and the owner of the ranch, read to them the story of the birth of the Christ Child. He then asked Clark to lead them in prayer. Some throats were self-consciously cleared and many gazes were fastened on the tops of boots or the big leathery hands in their laps, but everyone listened carefully.

The meal began in comparative silence, but it wasn't long until hearty laughter and good-natured teasing took over. Nathan and Josiah joined in merrily, describing in detail to the ranch hands their gifts of the morning, the trip to the barn with the new halter that "Spider liked real good," and their ride on Grandpa's sled.

After they all had eaten as much as they possibly could, the guests moved to the living room where a friendly fire welcomed them. Henry was not there to lead them with his guitar, having decided to follow the LaHaye tradition and have a family Christmas dinner for his own hands. But, in spite of the absence of Henry, they sang the Christmas carols under Willie's direction. Those who did not sing seemed to enjoy listening.

Scottie was the first who had to leave. He always took responsibility for the Christmas shift with the cattle. Usually one or two of the other hands joined him voluntarily out of respect for their boss. Today it was Jake and Charlie. Lane announced that he planned to ride over to the doctor's to see how Jedd was doing. Clark said that he would like to go with him.

The cowboys left, calling their thanks as they flipped their stetsons back onto their heads. The two little boys were tucked in for a much-needed nap. Missie and Marty went to help Wong and Cookie clear the dishes, and the house again fell into silence.

The ride through the crisp afternoon was cold for Clark and Lane. Clark especially noticed it in the stump of his missing leg. He had not thought to provide extra protection for the area and found that it was very sensitive to the cold. Lane, without saying anything, swung down from his horse and pulled a blanket from behind his saddle. Speaking of other things, he crossed to Clark's horse and tucked the blanket around the stump, making sure that it was fastened securely in place and would not slip with the movement of horse and rider. Still making no reference to the missing leg or the blanket, he remounted and they moved on. Clark was much more comfortable on the remainder of the ride.

They found Jedd in much the same condition as he had been the night before. Señora De la Rosa sat with him. Jedd had been bathed and his beard and hair had been neatly trimmed. His feet and hands bore large bandages, and Clark was reminded of the doctor's concern for the fingers and toes that had been frozen. When they found that Jedd was not conscious, they did not stay long. The doctor promised that if the man roused, he would send one of his ranch hands with the message. The doctor seemed encouraged that Jedd had held his own throughout the day. His pulse rate had improved somewhat, and this gave Juan some hope.

Lane and Clark left for home after sharing a cup of hot coffee and some of Maria's special Christmas baking.

As they mounted, Clark tucked Lane's blanket around himself.

"Never knowed," he said simply, "jest how much the cold would bother a leg like mine. Here I was a pridin' myself thet I wouldn't be sufferin' with any cold toes on this here side."

Lane smiled but only said, "It'll toughen."

Chapter Twenty-eight

From Death to Life

It was three days before a rider came from the De la Rosas' and said that Jedd Larson was now awake. Clark immediately saddled a horse and prepared to go to him. He tucked his well-worn Bible inside his jacket and asked Marty for an extra blanket.

"It's a trick I learned from Lane," explained Clark in answer to her unasked question. "This here short leg gets awful cold. A blanket keeps it more livable."

Marty spent the day knitting and praying. It seemed that Clark was gone forever, but at last Marty heard the sound of a horse approaching the barn. In the clear, crisp winter air, the sounds of the hoofbeats rang out clearly. Max left the yard on the run, always the first to welcome a rider.

Marty watched from the window until Clark came in sight, and then she grabbed her shawl and ran to meet him.

"Come to Missie's," she called. "She'll want to hear all 'bout it, too."

Clark changed direction and headed for the big house as

Marty ran down the rutted, snowpacked path to meet him there.

"Oh, I was hopin' thet you'd come right on over here," Missie called to them from the doorway. "I jest couldn't wait to hear all 'bout it."

Missie led the way to the open fire. "We're near bustin'," she spoke for both of them. "Tell us 'bout it quick."

"Did Jedd know ya this time?" interposed Marty.

"Oh, he knew me all right. Was 'most as surprised to see me as I was to see him the other night."

"What did he say?"

"He asked first thing 'bout the girls."

Marty's eyes misted. "I'm so glad thet he cares somethin' fer 'em," she said.

"He seemed right concerned. Said thet he had made up his mind to go on home. He was tryin' to reach town an' the train station when he got lost in the snow an' stranded out on the range."

"Did he mention Tina again?"

"We talked 'bout Tina quite a piece."

Marty could wait no longer. "Clark," she said, "were ya able to talk to 'im 'bout his need fer God?"

"I was. We went through the Bible 'most from cover to cover."

"Did he understand?"

"Seemed to."

"Did he . . . did he. . . ?"

Clark put his arm around his wife and pulled her close. His eyes blurred and his throat sounded hoarse. "Those girls of ours are gonna be happy to know thet their pa joined their ma today."

"Ya mean—?"

"Jedd Larson made his peace with his Savior."

"Oh, thank Ya, Father," prayed Marty, the tears spilling down her cheeks.

Clark cleared his throat.

"But he joined Tina in another way, too."

Marty and Missie waited, eyes wide.

"Jedd didn't make it," Clark said quietly. "Juan had to do surgery. Jedd wasn't strong enough to stand it. The frozen fingers and toes had turned bad; there wasn't any way thet Juan could save 'im. He's been stayin' with him day an' night, fightin' to bring 'im through this but—"

"But he did, Clark. He did!" exclaimed Marty. "Because of Juan's fight to save 'im, Jedd not only has life—but *everlastin'* life."

"I'm afraid thet a doctor doesn't look at things thet way," said Clark soberly.

"But it's true. And, oh, Clark, iffen you hadn't been here, Jedd maybe wouldn't have decided to make his peace with God 'fore he died." Marty's eyes fell to Clark's pant leg, pinned up securely just below the knee. "Iffen it wouldn't have been fer the accident, ya wouldn't have been here, Clark. We would have been gone home long ago."

Clark pulled her closer to him and kissed her hair.

Chapter Twenty-nine

Happenings

During the long winter days, Marty spent her time in the little soddy doing knitting, mending, or hand sewing for Missie and her family. She also had a basketful of socks to mend for the ranch hands, having made discreet inquiries after the Christmas sock-viewing. Clark used his hours to make things with his hands and his limited tools. In the long evenings, he spent hours with his Bible, studying for the Sunday lessons with the little congregation.

Each Sunday after the worshipers gathered together for their service, there were discussions concerning the materials and the progress of the church building. As the building committee continued planning and ordering supplies, the building was taking shape on paper and in the minds of the people, even though not a stake had been pounded or a nail driven. However, the materials were all being stockpiled at the Newtons' as they arrived by train, and a building bee was planned as soon as the weather would permit. Folks hoped for an early spring so that work might be started.

As the weather improved, so did the Sunday attendance. Once again, the folks from the town ventured forth. It was a long drive, but they seemed anxious to be a part of the fellowship and to keep informed about progress on the church building. Besides, they reported, though they enjoyed the Bible studies at home and it had been a good idea, it was not the same as meeting with the group and hearing Clark's insights on the truths from the scripture portion.

During the week, when Marty felt too confined, she would toss her shawl about her shoulders and hurry down the snow-crusted path to Missie's house. On a few occasions, Missie came to visit her while the children slept. Missie loved to sit in the quiet, snug little soddy, sipping tea with her mother. She realized that the days would quickly pass and Marty would all too soon return back home.

As the winter days lengthened, their visits turned to garden plans and spring setting hens. It was hard to stay in the house with the drifts of snow shrinking daily.

Clark, too, had been planning ahead, only his thoughts had taken a different turn. He thought often about the small congregation. He had enjoyed the opportunity to lead them over the winter months. He knew that they were not likely to soon find a minister for the group. What would happen when he had to leave for home? Clark decided to ride over and see Henry. And so it was that Clark began to have study sessions with Henry to prepare him to take over leadership of the church. The people must know that when Clark left there would still be worship and Bible study. The building was only a small part of the requirements for a congregation.

At long last, spring did arrive. This time it did not come slowly as spring so often does. One day it was still winter, and the next day spring was unmistakably in the air.

The spring birds appeared, little flowers colored the hillsides, green grass carpeted the area by the flowing spring, and Nathan ran capless and nursed a runny nose.

Missie's mind quickly switched to her planting. She pulled out all of her seeds, giving special attention to the ones that Clark and Marty had brought with them on the train. Scattering the little packages all across her table, she and her father began to sort and plan. Nathan and Josiah wished to get in on the activity, and soon her carefully sorted seeds were all mixed up again. Marty shepherded the boys to the kitchen for milk and cookies, and Clark and Missie continued their garden plans.

In spite of his crutch, it was Clark who cared for the plowing of the soil. He arranged little pots for planting inside seedlings and advised Missie as to what would grow best, where and when to plant it. Marty smiled as she watched father and daughter working together.

After the garden was started, it was time for Missie to turn to her chickens. She had spotted six hens with a desire to nest, and Missie carefully selected a setting of eggs for each one of them. Clark helped her with the coops, and the hens were housed in fine style. Missie placed her settings under the mothers-to-be and marked her calendar for the coming event.

The date for the church building bee was set. Wagons loaded with excited families, food and tools headed for the Newton's ranch. Cookie had to be available at home to feed the hands who were on duty with the cattle. Wong did not go either. He was not a builder and did not feel comfortable about sharing the cooking duties with several neighborhood women, so he stayed in his own kitchen and sent a big bucket of his special doughnuts to go with the morning coffee.

Juan had discovered two experienced carpenters from town who took charge of the actual construction. The neighborhood men offered their hands wherever they were needed.

Within the week, the church building was lifting its spire proudly toward the sky, the barren prairie and wide horizon making a dramatic silhouette. Señora De la Rosa wept the first time she heard the bell peal, reaching across the miles without even echoing from the distant hills.

The first service in the new church was announced. Many new faces appeared in the congregation that day. Clark wondered, as he looked over the crowd, how many were there for social reasons or idle curiosity and how many were true worshipers "in spirit and in truth." Regardless of their purpose, he saw a real opportunity to open the Word of God to them.

Marty sat with Missie and her family on one of the new pews, Nathan tucked in between them and Josiah snuggled on his mother's lap. *I love the smell of new wood,* thought Marty as she looked around at the ones nearby and sensed their joyful anticipation. *While we've been here,* her thoughts moved on, *God has provided a doctor for their bodies' needs and a church for their spiritual needs. Thank Ya, Lord!*

Clark was pleased to see quite a few of the new people continue to come as the Sundays passed one by one. The church members made it a point to keep in contact with all who had visited the church.

Nathan and Josiah now spent much of their time outside during the lovely spring weather. They had planted, with the help of their grandfather, their own small garden and daily checked it for progress, then would run with reports to their grandmother.

"It's growin'!" cried Nathan one day as he burst in upon Marty.

"What's growin'?" she asked innocently.

"My garden! Come see. Come see."

Marty hurried after him. Nathan fell on his knees and pointed to some small, green plants just beginning to poke their heads out of the soil. Marty didn't have the heart to tell him just then that they were weeds. *Wait until some real garden begins to grow,* she told herself, *and then we'll care fer the weeds.*

But Josiah cared for many of them. He pulled them up to see how they were doing, then pushed them awkwardly into the ground again and pounded them on their tender tops with his pudgy palm—even the hardy weeds did not survive his "tender" care.

Eventually the "real gardens" did begin to grow. Marty was not sure who was the most excited with their growing plants—the two small boys or Missie. Marty understood. She wished she were home planting her own garden. She missed it and wondered if Ellie and the boys would be taking care of it.

Marty took another horseback ride out with Missie and the

boys to view the herds. Hundreds of spring calves scampered around their bawling mothers. Marty had never seen such a sight.

Nathan climbed down off his pony to pick wild flowers for his two favorite ladies. Marty's smile swept from him to Missie who sat on her horse with the young Josiah astraddle the saddle in front of her. Missie's face was flushed, her figure gently rounding with the new life growing inside her, and her hair, teased loose by the prairie wind, fanned about her. Behind her, the hills rolled on and on like a gently dipping brownish-green sea. Beyond them, friendly mountains lifted silver peaks to play secret games with the fluffy clouds that hung low in the sky. The scene was lovely, full of life and warmth and love, and a memory that Marty would cherish for many years to come.

She was thankful that Missie and Willie had come west. She was glad that she and Clark had been able to visit; she was even glad for the extra time that Clark's accident had allowed them. Missie was happy here. As Marty looked at her contented daughter, she realized that Missie really belonged here. She was a gentle part of Willie's West. Marty looked about her with new appreciation for the ever-present hills and the openness—even the wind. This land spoke of freedom, of independence and of strength. Marty was proud that her daughter was a part of it.

They rode home in silence . . . each one thinking thoughts that belonged to herself. Nathan cantered on ahead on his Spider, manfully "breaking trail" for his mother and grandmother. Josiah, his head resting against his mother, nodded off to sleep.

Clark was waiting for them when they returned. He had spent the day putting new legs on Cookie's worktable.

"How did you an' Cookie make out?" asked Missie, knowing that Clark had been looking for an opportunity for a heart-to-heart talk with Cookie about his relationship with God.

Clark shook his head. "We had a good talk—nice an' open—but Cookie is still hesitant. He says thet he wants to be sure he is acceptin' Jesus Christ—not Clark Davis."

"I don't understand," said Missie.

Marty thought about the statement for a moment. "I think maybe I do," she said slowly.

"Well," said Clark modestly, "Cookie says thet he admires me . . . guess 'cause we both of us had the same kind of accident. Not much to admire a man fer, but Cookie reasons a little different than some men do. Anyway, he listens to the Word as I give it Sunday by Sunday; he sees me able to make do with one leg. . . . I don't know. He's got it all mixed up as to what I can do as a man and what I can do with the Lord's help. He's not sure yet where the difference lies. Cookie's right, ya know. I don't want him to be a follower of Clark Davis. Iffen he can't find the difference here, then he should wait until he does. No good followin' a man. Nothin' thet I can give to Cookie thet he can't find in hisself."

"Sounds strange to me," mused Missie. "I never thought of anyone getting mixed up on man-followin' before. Seems to me it should be plain as can be that Jesus is the only way to heaven."

"I left Cookie my Bible and marked some verses for 'im to read. I hope thet he will be able to understand their meanin'."

"We're gonna have to do some prayin'," Missie said simply as Clark and Nathan moved away with the horses and she and Marty walked on to the house, the sleeping Josiah in her arms. "Iffen Pa can't make Cookie see the difference, how will Willie or Henry ever do it?"

It was Lane who showed Cookie the difference. He walked into the cookshack and found Cookie frowning over Clark's Bible.

"I still don't figure it," mumbled Cookie.

"Don't figure what?" asked Lane, reaching for the ever-ready coffeepot.

"Iffen I take on this here religion, will I be doin' it to try to become a man like Clark Davis?"

"What's wrong with bein' a man like Clark Davis?"

"Nothin'. Nothin' thet I can see. Only he says thet tryin' to be like 'im ain't gonna git me one step closer to those pearly gates yer always talkin' 'bout."

"Oh, thet," said Lane, understanding Cookie's dilemma. "He's right."

"But how can I be like *Jesus*?" asked Cookie in frustration. "I don't even know *Him*."

"Forgit 'bout bein' *like Him* fer now," said Lane. "Yer tryin' to start too far ahead of yerself." Cookie looked doubtful but let Lane continue.

"You've heard it preached an' read many times thet all men are sinners?"

"Yah," grunted Cookie.

"Are ya a-doubtin' thet ya fit in thet category?"

"Shucks, no," said Cookie. "I know myself better'n thet."

"Okay," said Lane, "thet's where ya start. Now ya know thet yer a sinner, an' I guess iffen yer wantin' to copy after Davis, ya don't really want to stay one."

Cookie nodded his agreement.

"Well, how ya try to clean up yer act ain't gonna make a whole lot of difference. You'll never measure up, no matter how hard ya try. Oh, ya might even git to *act* as good as Clark Davis himself, but thet won't really impress God none. He still sees deeper than the skin.

"Bible says thet man looks on the outside but God looks on the heart. Also says thet the heart of man is 'desperately wicked.' But the good news is thet our hearts can be changed. Now, thet there's the startin' place.

"Jesus, holy an' pure, died fer every dirty, wicked heart thet ever beat. All we gotta do is see what we are, an' who He is, an' accept fer ourselves what He did. Thet's all there is to it. From there on, He does the workin' on makin' ya a follower."

Cookie's eyes opened wide at the simplicity of it. Lane gulped the last of his coffee, placed his cup on the table, and headed for the door.

When he reached the door he hesitated, turned to Cookie, and said softly, "All ya gotta do is ask Him."

After Lane was gone, Cookie did.

Chapter Thirty

Plans

Clark and Marty began to make plans for going home, talking quietly together in the privacy of the little soddy. At first it was like a dream to be thinking of boarding the slow-moving train again and leaving behind the West that they had come to respect and the family that they loved so deeply. Marty wished there was a way that she could bundle them all up and take them home with her. But then she thought of Willie and his love for his spread, Missie and the sun reflecting in her eyes, and Nathan and Josiah as they rushed about their beloved hills with the wind whipping at their hair; and she knew that she would not want to pick them up by their roots and try to transplant them—not really.

Marty's thoughts turned more and more to her farm-home family. *How's Clare and his young Kate doin' in the little log house? Is Arnie still seein' the preacher's daughter? What is the girl really like? Is Ellie entertainin' any gentleman callers? Which of the neighborhood young men will be the first one to notice our pretty young daughter who is now a woman?* She wondered if Luke still nursed his dream of going off to train as a doctor and how Dr. Watkins and the boy were getting along. Marty was anxious to get home again and have some of her questions answered.

A long letter from Ellie arrived. She told about the new grass and leaves on the flowering shrubs. She spoke of the songbirds that were back and the new colt in the pasture. She reported that Clare had plowed the garden spot and she and Kate had planted the garden—more than they would ever be using themselves, she was sure, but they just couldn't seem to get stopped once they had started. She told of Nandry's tears of joy and sorrow upon receiving the news of her father. She wrote that Nandry had immediately sat down and penned a long letter to Clae and Joe. Ellie gave news about the neighbors, the church, and the school. But she did not say how Clare and Kate were doing in the little house, nor if Arnie was still seeing the preacher's daughter, nor if she, Ellie, was receiving gentleman callers, nor how Luke was doing in his quest of becoming a doctor. Marty's heart yearned to know all the answers.

"Clark," she said, folding up the letter for the third time, "I think thet it be time we got us some tickets."

Clark ran a hand over the rope that he was braiding for Nathan and agreed. "Yah," he said, "I think thet it be. We best have us a chat with Willie an' Missie tonight."

That evening Marty expected some protests when they voiced their decision. Missie set down the cup of coffee she had just poured and took a deep breath.

"No use pretendin' that we didn't know it had to come," she said quietly. "No use fussin' 'bout it. You must be powerful lonesome for the ones at home. I marvel that you were able to stay away this long." She poured another cup of coffee and handed it to Willie. " 'Course I wish you could just stay on here forever. I know better. Truth is, I'm thankful for every day we have already had."

Willie cleared his throat and ran a hand through his heavy head of hair. "Don't know as how I'm gonna git along without yer pair of hands," he said to Clark. "Can't believe the number of little things thet you've seen to over the winter

206

months—things thet none of us ever seemed to find time fer."

Clark smiled. "Got a good idea," he said. "Why don't I see iffen I can talk yer pa into comin' out fer a spell? He's awful handy 'round a place. Never seed a man thet could make things look better in short order than yer pa. How 'bout it?"

Willie grinned. "I'd like thet," he said sincerely. "Seems to have been a long time since I seen my pa."

"When do you plan on goin'?" asked Missie.

"I'll be a-ridin' into town tomarra and checkin' out the trains. No use waitin' 'til it gits so hot thet one can hardly stand the ride. It was pretty hot at times when we came out last year. Thought thet it might be a little cooler iffen we go right away."

Missie was silent.

Marty looked at her daughter and caught her blinking away tears.

"We've loved havin' you," Missie finally managed. "You know that. Just sorry we have to send you back to the rest of the family different than you came, Pa. Hope that they won't hold it against us and the West."

"Why should they?" asked Clark. "Accidents aren't confined to one place. Jest before we left home, a neighbor farmer got drug by a team of horses and lost both of his legs."

"Still," said Missie, "it's gonna be a shock for them."

"We're gonna miss ya at the church," put in Willie. "Can't believe how much interest there is since we started to have real services."

"Thet won't stop," Clark answered. "Henry is all prepared to give ya Bible lessons jest as I was doin'. He'll do a fine job. I already wrote to Joe to send Henry out some good Bible books fer studyin'. I expect Henry to really git into 'em. He loves studyin' the Word and will bring to the people everything thet he can find. I think thet Henry is gonna make a fine lay preacher."

"We're glad for Henry," Missie said. "He's been a great help and a good friend ever since we left home."

"Ya have some very fine neighbors here," Marty said with feeling. "I'm so relieved, Missie, to know that ya have ladies to visit and share with and a good doctor close by so thet ya won't need to go way up to Tettsford Junction fer this next little one."

"So am I," Missie agreed, reaching out to take Willie's hand. "That was what I hated most 'bout havin' Nathan an' Josiah—the long months of bein' away from Willie."

"Well, iffen I'm gonna make thet ride into town tomarra, I guess I should be gittin' to bed. Thet's a long way fer a slow rider to be a travelin'." Clark stood and lifted his crutch into position.

"Would ya prefer the team to a saddle horse?" asked Willie.

"Hey, thet sounds like a good idea. Might be I'll even take young Nathan along with me, iffen his mother agrees."

"He'd love to go," said Missie. "He's gonna really miss you. Both of you. He won't know what to do with himself when you leave."

"Won't be long until Nathan will be needin' school. Any plans?" asked Marty.

"Willie and some of the neighbor men are meetin' at Juan's on Wednesday night. There are several families whose children are much older than Nathan, and they are most anxious to get them some learnin' before they're so old that they think they don't even *need* school."

"Glad to hear thet."

"The church committee is goin' to tell them they can meet in the church if they want to."

"Thet's a good idea," said Clark with enthusiasm. "I sure hope thet it all works out fer 'em. Now, we better git. I'll be by to pick up yer son 'bout eight, iffen thet's all right."

"That'll be fine. He'll be up an' ready to go. Why don't you both come on over an' have breakfast with us first?"

"Oh, no, dear, we don't want—"

"Ma," said Missie, "please. There won't be too many days for us to be a-sharin' our time together. Let's make the most of them."

Marty kissed her daughter and agreed on breakfast the next morning.

Chapter Thirty-one

Farewells

Clark and Nathan enjoyed a leisurely drive into town. Nathan, curious about everything that he heard and saw, kept up an excited stream of questions and comments. Clark realized that the young boy was truly ready for school.

"What ya plannin' to be when ya grow up, boy?" asked Clark.

"I don't know, Grandpa. Some days I wanna be a rancher like my pa. An' sometimes I wanna be a foreman like Scottie, an' some days I wanna be a cowboy like Lane, but most of all I think I wanna be a cook like Cookie."

Clark laughed. The ranch was really all of the life that the boy knew. Clark determined to send Nathan a packet of good books.

"What do you wanna be, Grandpa?"

"Ya mean when I grow up?"

"Yer already growed."

"Oh, yah," said Clark, "I guess I am at that."

"What ya gonna be?" asked Nathan again.

"Well," said Clark, "I'm a farmer."

"What do farmers do?"

"Much like a rancher, only they don't raise quite so many cows and horses. And they might have pigs or sheep or even goats to go with their other animals. And they plow fields, an' pick rock, an' pull stumps, an' plant grain thet they harvest every fall. Then they build haystacks and store feed fer their animals to eat in the winter months. And they butcher an' cure meat, an' chop wood, an' doctor sick critters, an' take in garden vegetables, an' fix fence."

"Boy," said Nathan, "farmers do lots of stuff, huh, Grandpa?"

"Guess we do."

"Can ya do all thet, Grandpa?"

"Shore. Don't take nobody special to do all thet."

"Boy, ya can do lots of things with only one leg, can't ya, Grandpa?"

"Well, ya see, son, when I was doin' all those things I still had me two legs. So I been thinkin' some lately of how I can still do the same things. It's gonna take some special equipment. Ya know the piece of harness that I made fer myself so I could balance and still handle the horse an' the plow?" Nathan nodded, remembering the funny contraption his grandfather had used.

"Well, I plan on buildin' a lot of things like thet. I couldn't start to work on them yet, 'cause they've got to be measured jest so, to fit the different things thet I be usin'—like the plow an' the rake an' the seeder. I'm gonna make 'em all when I git home. I got this here idea of how I'll fix the plow, see—" And Clark commenced to tell Nathan his idea, Nathan's eyes becoming big as he listened. The miles melted by as the two worked together on Clark's plans.

Clark discovered that the next suitable train left the following Tuesday. He made plans for their tickets and then took Nathan to the General Store for a treat. They also pocketed some sweets for Josiah and then headed the team for home.

The news of the upcoming departure had Marty in a flurry. She felt that she had so much to do to prepare for the journey, but when she set about to do it she found that it wasn't so much after all—not nearly what it had been in preparing for their trip out to Missie. There was only their own luggage to care for since all of the things they had brought west for Missie and the family would be staying right there. Marty relaxed and enjoyed her last days by spending them with the boys just as much as she could.

She cleaned out the tiny soddy and bade it a fond farewell, then moved their things back into Missie's fine house for the remaining days.

Willie came home from the De la Rosas' with exciting news. The community had voted to begin the new school in the church building. Henry's Melinda had been asked to teach. Her close neighbor, Mrs. Netherton, an older woman with no children, had agreed to stay with Melinda's young son while she was at school. Since Melinda was reluctant to leave her boy behind, the first year of school would be held only for three days a week. Still, the neighborhood agreed that this arrangement was far better than no school at all.

Willie and Missie decided that Nathan would be allowed to join the school-bound crowd. As Melinda would be driving right by their ranch, she agreed to pick up the young scholar.

Marty took special note of each day as it ticked by. A little clock ran in her mind: *This is our last Friday . . . our last Saturday . . . our last service in the little church.* She prepared with extra care. Clark had already shared with her some of his thoughts on the scripture portion for the day. Marty felt them to be most appropriate on their last day with the congregation that they had learned to love. There was no better message that Clark could leave with them.

When Clark stood before the group on that last Sunday, he read solemnly, yet triumphantly, from the Word: "Thus saith the Lord, Let not the wise man glory in his wisdom, neither let the mighty man glory in his might, let not the rich man glory in his riches: but let him that glorieth glory in this, that he understandeth and knoweth me, that I am the Lord which exercise lovingkindness, judgment, and righteousness, in the earth: for in these things I delight, saith the Lord" (Jer. 9:23,

24). As she listened, Marty prayed for each individual who sat in the seats around her. Her desire, and Clark's, was that each one of them might deeply live the truth of the Scripture, this one in particular.

After the service had ended, Clark asked Henry to speak to the congregation. It was common knowledge that when Clark left, Henry would be leading the group.

With tears in his voice, he expressed his thanks to Clark and to Marty for their leadership and encouragement over the months they had been with them, the congregation echoing his appreciation. Then Clark and Marty, taken completely by surprise, were guests of honor as the whole fellowship gathered around to give them a farewell party. Food was spread out on makeshift tables, and ladies served while the men and children dug in with relish. Underlying the festivities and laughter was a feeling of sadness because of the fact that in just two days the Davises would be leaving them. Clark and Marty appreciated each one who came with a special thank-you shining from his or her eyes and warm handshakes. They were special, these people. They were special because they were Christian brothers and sisters. Clark and Marty both knew they would miss them.

Chapter Thirty-two

Homeward Bound

When Tuesday arrived, Marty was packed and ready to go. Willie brought around the team and, as Missie prepared her sons for the trip to town and Clark went to say a last farewell to the ranch hands, Marty slipped out of the house and made one last trip to the little soddy.

She was not as nostalgic about the small shack for her own sake as for Missie's. Marty had spent the one winter in the soddy by choice. Missie had made it a home because it was all that was available to her.

Marty stood and gazed around the little room once again. In her fancy she could see Missie as a very young bride bending over the tiny stove with its cow-chip fire, preparing the evening meal. In the cradle at the end of the bed would rest the tiny baby, Nathan. Willie would return from his long, hard day of herding cattle to be greeted with love and concern and a simple meal.

Marty could picture, too, the growing Nathan, the Christmas gathering of ranch hands, the visits with new neighbors.

Marty would cherish her mental pictures of the little shack. Her own winter spent there helped her to more clearly picture Missie in the soddy.

Yes, she and Clark had been happy in the soddy, too. Those long evenings as she sat sewing and Clark pored over his Bible, sharing with her special truths as he found them and getting her thoughts on particular verses—these were memories to treasure. Perhaps it would be many days until she and Clark would have so many hours of each day to cherish as their own without interruption from the daily demands of farm and family.

Marty retraced her steps to the house—Missie's beautiful home. Marty had never seen a home that was more comfortable or more tasteful. She was proud of Missie and her homemaking ability.

They were loading the wagon when Marty rounded the corner. She stepped forward to take her place. All the ranch hands who were not on duty were present to shake her hand, and Marty spoke to each of them. Cookie was the last in the line.

The old ranch cook stepped forward, his hand outstretched.

"Cookie," said Marty, with tears in her eyes, "we are jest so thankful to God fer yer choosin' to follow Him. Ya're jest so special to us in so many ways."

Cookie changed his mind and gave Marty an affectionate hug instead.

Lane moved forward and took Clark's hand. He said nothing in words, but his eyes spoke volumes.

Just as the wagon was about to move out of the yard, Wong came running, waving a bundle in his hands. It was some of his fresh doughnuts, a treat for the trip. Marty and Clark thanked him warmly and he beamed as he bobbed his head.

"Much thanks," he said. "Much thanks for the special joy that you brought to this house and to Wong's kitchen. Come again, maybe?"

The wagon pulled away amid hat-waving and calls, and then they were on their way.

Marty's view was blurred with tears as she looked back from the hillside where she had taken her first look at Missie's home. So much had happened there to endear so many people to her heart.

Josiah crawled on her knees, and she held him close all of the way to town. Nathan chattered excitedly, feeling that Grandma and Grandpa were privileged indeed to be passengers on a real, moving train.

"An' someday I'm gonna come all the way on the train to the farm an' see ya," he promised.

And Josiah echoed, "See ya."

"Yah," said Nathan, "me and Joey. We'll come an' see ya."

"That would be wonderful," said Marty and held her "Joey" even closer.

When they reached the town, Clark checked their trunk through, and they gathered their hand-baggage and went to get a cup of coffee while they waited for the train.

It was hard to know what should be said in their last few minutes together. It seemed that there was still so much to say, in spite of the fact that they had spent months talking.

They filled the time with small talk and reminders of messages for each one of the family members on the farm.

It was time to leave when Scottie appeared.

"I wasn't able to see ya off at the house," he said, extending his hand to Clark, "but I shore didn't want to miss sayin' a good-bye. Guess I needn't say thet we are gonna miss ya 'round the spread. S'pose now I'll have to mend my own halters and clean my own barns."

Clark smiled. He didn't feel he had helped Scottie that much, but he knew that what he had done had been appreciated. He shook Scottie's hand firmly. "Ya'll always have a warm spot in our hearts an' prayers," he told the ranch foreman, and Scottie smiled.

They walked slowly to the train station. Already the train was sending up great puffs of smoke as the firebox was filled in preparation for the departure. Long cars were filled with bawling steers, and Marty knew that they would share the ride with many cattle heading for market. She wondered if some of Willie's herd might be on board.

It was time for the last tearful good-bye.

"Pa," spoke Missie, her voice choked, "ya s'pose thet ya could be shippin' me out some apple cuttin's by train? I've been missin' 'em something awful."

Clark was thoughtful. He wasn't sure that apple trees would grow in the area, but he nodded his head to affirm his answer. "Why not?" he said. "It's shore worth a try. Ya can plant them down by yer spring an' make sure thet they git plenty of water. Might not produce too much fruit, but ya might git enough fer a pie or two."

Missie laughed through her tears. "Truth is," she stated, "I won't even be carin' too much if I don't get fruit. It's the blossoms thet I miss the most. Seems they promise spring, an' love, an' happiness, ever'time they appear."

Clark gave his daughter an understanding hug.

They all embraced one last time and told one another again how much the visit had meant to each one of them. Marty and Clark held their two grandsons for as long as they dared; and then the "all aboard" was called, they waved one last time, and climbed on the train.

Marty waved until the train turned a curve and then the town and her family were left behind. She then wiped her tears on her handkerchief and resolved that she would cry no more.

The day dragged by, measured by the rhythms of the steel wheels. Each revolution took them farther away from Willie and Missie, but closer to the other members of their family.

There were a few stops at small towns here and there— some of them seeming to take far too long—but then they traveled on again, day and night. On the third day, they pulled into the town where they had switched trains on their westward journey. Again it meant an overnight stay. Clark and Marty both remembered the dirty little hotel and its bedbugs. "Surely we can do better than thet," Clark assured Marty, and made some discreet inquiries. They were pointed to an elderly lady's house whom, they were told, kept roomers on occasion; fortunately, the woman had room and accepted them as overnight guests.

By the time they neared the station the next morning, shoppers were beginning to appear on the streets. The town was again awakening as it had done the year before.

When they reached the train station, Clark held the door for Marty and she passed through and headed for some seats near the window. She would just sit and wait while Clark checked out the departure time.

Clark walked closely behind her to settle the luggage that he carried, before going to the ticket counter. Other passengers milled about the room as well.

Marty heard the loud voice of a youngster. "Ma, look—look at thet poor man."

Marty's head came up slowly and she looked around her, already feeling pity in her heart for some unfortunate person.

She spotted no one.

"Ya lookin' fer the man?"

At the sound of Clark's voice, Marty flushed, embarrassed to be caught staring about because of curiosity. Her eyes admitted to Clark that, indeed, she had been looking for "the poor man."

Clark was quick to ease her guilt.

"I was, too," he confessed. "Did ya spot 'im?"

Marty shook her head no.

"Me neither," said Clark and then began to chuckle.

Marty looked at him in surprise.

"Thet is," went on Clark, " 'til I looked at myself."

"Yerself?"

Clark chuckled again.

"He was talkin' 'bout *me*, Marty."

"You?"

Then Marty's gaze fell to the pinned-up empty pant leg and the crutch held in Clark's hand. Her breath caught in a little gasp. It was true. The boy was speaking of Clark—and Clark was chuckling!

Then Marty saw it—the humor of it, the glory of it. They both had completely forgotten that Clark was considered handicapped—"the poor man." They reached for one another and laughed together, tears of joy running freely down their cheeks.